I0731611

MINIONS AND MAGIC

ACCIDENTAL WITCHES BOOK 5

DEBRA DUNBAR

debra dunbar
FIENDISHLY FUN FICTION

Copyright © 2019 by Debra Dunbar

All rights reserved.

No part of this book may be reproduced in any form or by any electronic or mechanical means, including information storage and retrieval systems, without written permission from the author, except for the use of brief quotations in a book review.

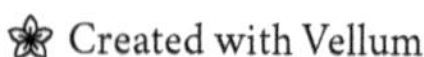 Created with Vellum

CHAPTER 1

XAVIER

I'll admit that Benjamin Frederick Allen threw one heck of an engagement party, but then again he could afford to. The man had made millions over the last decade. Everything he touched turned to gold, just like Midas. And just like Midas, that gift had come with a price.

I was here to remind him of that price—and to remind him that the poorly worded bargain he'd made ten years ago at a crossroads didn't mean the money he so desperately desired would bring him any happiness.

His lover had given him the clap. His wife had left him. He'd had ten years of IRS audits, and was facing a class-action lawsuit. He was completely unaware that the seam in his pants had split and everyone was getting a lovely view of his red underwear. In addition, the daughter whose engagement party he'd spent some serious coin on hated him and was eagerly counting the days until he died.

That one wasn't my doing. I too was eagerly counting the days until Benjamin Frederick Allen died, but for different reasons. I'd get his soul—a far more valuable commodity than a bunch of paper that the government would seize less than a year after his death.

What to do, what to do? Hmmm.

I'd thought about bringing an unexpected tornado to ruin this party, but that was too much work. So here I stood, looking quite dapper if I might say so myself, wearing a tuxedo and holding a glass of expensive champagne, trying to decide the best way to make Benjamin Frederick Allen just a little more miserable. He was going to die in two years, so I really needed to step up my game before he was out of my hands and into someone else's in hell.

The food.

I felt a twinge of guilt, because the food really looked magnificent. Maybe I wouldn't tamper with all of it. I sauntered over to the tables and eyed the spread. Prime rib sandwiches with fresh horseradish. Bite-size quiche with spinach. Little pastries with bresaola and blue cheese. Lamb meatballs with feta. Hand-made potato chips sprinkled with Old Bay seasoning. A mushroom pâté with bread that smelled like it had come right out of the oven. Tiny crab cakes that looked as if there was barely enough filler to hold them together. Colorful macarons. Cups with dark chocolate mousse. Cupcakes with rich buttercream. A ginger cake with a spicy aroma that made my mouth water.

Messing with any of this would be a sin, but I was all about sin. Making a decision, I reached out to put my finger on the ginger cake and nearly leapt out of my skin when someone smacked my hand.

"Oh no you don't."

A woman stood next to me in a neatly pressed apron, a white chef's hat askew on her auburn hair. She waved a finger in my face—actually waved a finger in *my* face.

"I see you. I know what you are, and what you're about. No demon is gonna mess with my food. So you just back yourself away from the table and take your mischief elsewhere."

I'll admit I stood there gaping like an idiot, partly because she was beautiful, partly because she had the effrontery to smack my hand and order me around, and partly because she was a witch.

A witch. I hadn't come across one in centuries. I'd thought that they'd died out until word went around hell that Lucien had bonded with one.

A witch.

"Sorry." I was apologizing. Why was I apologizing? I never apologized. "It looks really good. Is there fresh ginger in it?"

She sniffed, folding her arms across her chest. "Of course there is. It's my own recipe."

Pride. I got a grip on myself and tried to act more like the powerful crossroads demon I was and less like a child who'd been caught trying to sneak a cookie. I could deal with pride. It was my favorite sin.

"I haven't had a chance to try anything yet." I gave her my sexiest smile. "Maybe you could prepare a plate for me since I seem to be forbidden from touching any of the food myself."

A blush rose up her neck and across her round face, making the smattering of freckles on her cheekbones disappear. For a second I thought she would comply, but then she shook her head and glared.

"Why are you here? I doubt Mr. Allen invited a demon to his daughter's engagement party."

"No, but Benjamin Frederick Allen made a deal with me ten years ago, and ever since that point, I have an automatic invitation to anywhere he may be—whether that's the boardroom, or the bathroom, or a party at his luxurious estate."

She appeared a bit taken aback at my words. "The *bath-*

room? You seriously spy on him when he's soaping up his nether parts in the shower, or taking a number two? Why the heck would you do that?"

I blinked, a little shocked that she was more concerned about my violating a human's expectation of privacy while cleaning himself or eliminating than that I was a demon who'd made a deal for a man's soul.

"Umm, well sometimes I make him drop the soap and whack his knee on the faucet when he bends over to get it. Or I make him slip and go down on his ass while getting out of the tub. And constipation or a burning sensation when someone goes wee is definitely on my list of favorites."

Wee. I'd actually said "wee" to this woman as if I needed to curtail my language in her presence. I was a demon. I could curse if I wanted to. And I'd just said "ass" so there was no need for me to use such an infantile euphemism as "wee".

"Those are spelled out in your contracts as liberties you can take when someone makes a deal with you?" She shook her head, her disgusted impression making my stomach twist into a nervous knot.

"No, they're not spelled out in the contract. That's the point. Broadly worded, sweeping contracts allow me a lot of latitude. Basically I get to do whatever I want to the person while they're still alive as long as they get whatever they traded their soul for."

She shook her head, mouth tight with disapproval. "Well, I don't think that sounds right. And what happens after these people die? Do you torture them with more than constipation and yeast infections?"

I shrugged. "Once they die, it's all out of my hands. My job is done. Their soul goes on to some other demon in hell. I don't bother myself with the administrative policy of what soul goes where and to who for what punishment. All I do is make the deals, deliver the requested wish, then make whatever remains of their lives miserable."

She didn't look particularly impressed by any of that. I clearly wasn't making a good impression on this witch, and for some crazy reason that bothered me. I wanted her to like me. I wanted her to find me clever and funny, smart and resourceful. Yeah. Crazy, I know.

"So Mr. Allen sold his soul to you? For what?" The witch asked.

I waved my hand around at the largesse. "What do you think? Money. It's the usual request. That and sex."

The woman's eyebrows shot up. "He seriously didn't earn this money?"

I shrugged. "Well, technically I guess he did. But it never would have happened if I hadn't intervened. Benjamin Frederick Allen may have been upper middle class without the deal he struck, but no mansion, no yacht, no private jet, no daughter-marrying-a-trust-fund-heir." I sent another slow, sexy smile her way. "No amazing catering of this party by a truly talented chef."

Her arms remained across her chest. "You haven't eaten anything yet. It might taste like my smoothies for all you know."

I had no idea what smoothies had to do with anything. Did she not *like* smoothies? Did she lack the ability to make one? Because I couldn't imagine how someone who could cook all this could screw up a simple blended beverage.

"Well," I tried the sexy smile again, "I would *love* to eat something, if only someone would stop smacking my fingers when I attempt it."

Her eyes narrowed. "I see auras, I'll have you know. You weren't going to eat that ginger cake, you were going to put some demon spell on it. Make it rot, or taste like dust, or give everyone who ate it explosive diarrhea or something."

It wasn't as if I'd lied to her. Maybe. I couldn't really remember half the time when I had told a lie. But either way, I really did want to try the cake, and a few of these other foods. Suddenly the day was less about ruining Benjamin Frederick Allen's life and more about this witch.

She regarded me for a moment then slid a slice of the cake onto a plate, handing it to me with a fork. I took a bite and had to pause to savor the texture and flavors before swallowing. Moist with a delicate crumb, the cake had the refreshing tang of fresh ginger tempered with a hint of vanilla, and balanced with a shadowy trace of Ceylonese cinnamon. And the icing… It had the richness of buttercream without the sweetness. I'd thought it was cream cheese, but it lacked the signature sour notes of that frosting.

It was magic. Once more I looked at the witch before me with her red hair and freckles, with the smug satisfied smile of someone who knew how good her culinary skills truly were. Pride. It was the best sin of all and it made my heart sing to see such a thing in her.

I wanted her. I wanted her magic sizzling against my skin. I wanted her body and her soul. I wanted her in my bed, by my side. I wanted her for all eternity. I was a crossroads demon, and all I desired was only one bargain away.

But first I needed to finish this slice of cake.

I swallowed that last amazing bite and was just about to wind up my pitch, when I found another plate in my hands. This one held the mushroom pâté surrounded by chunks of hearty bread.

It was a farmhouse style bread that had a thick crust with a faint dusting of flour and an uneven, bold crumb. I sniffed and caught a faint note of sourdough. Scooping up the pâté with a chunk of bread, I popped it into my mouth. The creamy-earthy complexity of the mushroom pâté mixed with the robust texture of the bread delivered a taste that angels would have described as heavenly.

I finished, and she shoved something else in my hands—a huge prime rib sandwich that took up the entire real estate of the tiny plate.

"Here. I need to get back to work. Help yourself to the food." She waved a stern finger under my nose. "But if I hear of one person getting sick, I'll hunt you down and lock you in a magical circle for the next two thousand years. Got it?"

I wanted to smile, but it wouldn't have been sexy at the moment given that my mouth was full of beef and sinus-cleansing horseradish. She was lying about the magical circle and the two thousand years thing, but she wasn't lying about hunting me down. The thought sent a rush of desire through me. I was tempted to see exactly what she *would* do with me if I tampered with her food.

But I had a better idea—one that would lead to a more mutually beneficial, long-term relationship with this witch than her trapping me with her magic. She'd be a worthy opponent, a tricky prey to catch, but I'd never lost a deal before and I was confident I wouldn't this time either.

I needed a plan. And I intended to get to work on one, just as soon as I finished this sandwich and ate some lamb meatballs as well as a few other things.

CHAPTER 2

GLENDA

A demon.

I tried really hard not to stare at him as I went about my duties, but he was always there in the corner of my vision.

Wow. Totally hot. I mean, smoking, inferno-of-hell hot.

Don't get me wrong, the demons who my sisters were bonded with were good-looking guys, but they did nothing for me. I'd just assumed maybe I wasn't into demons. I wasn't into a lot of possible romantic partners that I met—humans, shifters, vampires, fae, or any of the other supernatural beings who called Accident their home. Yeah, I'd dated a bit and even had a boyfriend or two throughout the years, but none of them had ever made my heart race the sort of giddy rhythm that this demon had.

Physically, he was a good-looking guy with golden-blond hair, bright blue eyes, and that self-assured, sexy smile that sent electricity zinging right down between my legs. I'd met lots of handsome men in my life, and none of them had rocked my world quite like this demon.

It wasn't just his muscles and gorgeous face. It was his

aura. Silver and black with swirls of orange. Looking at him with my second sight made me feel like I was staring down into an active volcano. Hot. Sexy.

And the best thing? He was scarfing down my food like a man who'd been living on cheap take-out for the last decade. I was a witch, but my greatest skills were in the kitchen. A man, or demon, that loved my cooking? *That* was the way to my heart.

Of course, everyone loved my cooking. People swooning over my custard creams led more to catering deals than dates, but a woman could always hope. And whether or not this demon was interested in things beyond my food, I still had a win here—he was completely ignoring his job duties and instead of making my client's life miserable, he was having a second helping of ginger cake.

Things got busy, and by the time the guests were beginning to filter out and I had started to clean up the empty trays and pans, the demon had left. Well, he'd left the food area where he'd stationed himself pretty much since he took that first taste of ginger cake. Just to make sure there was no mischief afoot that could tarnish my culinary reputation, I scanned the remaining crowd. Then I scanned once again using my second sight, just in case he'd changed forms.

Nope, no demon. My chest felt a little heavy to realize he truly was gone. Just like a hot guy to eat and run without even a thank-you. Figures.

I loaded the rest of the equipment into my van, cleaning the area and making some notes until Mr. Allen made his way over to me, check in hand. The man had always seemed polite and stately to me, and I admired that unlike most of my wealthy clients, he communicated with me himself rather than through an assistant or their party planner. Now I saw him through different eyes, looking at the lines around his mouth and the nervous tic at the corner of his eye. Had he really made a deal with a demon for his wealth?

The man handed me the check, which was made out for more than the contracted amount. "Thank you so much for today. The food was outstanding. Everyone raved about the cake and those little sandwiches. I'd worried there might be some...problem, but everything went off without a hitch."

His gaze darted around the manicured lawn, and I couldn't help but want to confirm what the demon had told me.

"You were worried about unwanted guests?" I smiled sympathetically. "An ex-boyfriend of your daughters with a grudge, perhaps?"

His laugh had a guilty edge to it. "No, more like an old business associate. I never invite him, but he has a habit of showing up and wrecking things. I thought maybe he was here earlier, but then nothing happened."

I was pretty sure if an old business associate had been crashing parties and harassing him, he would have had security here and a long-standing restraining order out on the guy. Unless, of course, the old business associate was a demon.

And if he couldn't keep a demon out of his bathroom, he didn't have any hope of keeping him away from a private party.

"There was a man who I'm pretty sure wasn't on the guest list." I forced a worried frown. "I made him a plate of food and kept an eye on him. He left a while ago."

I kept an eye on him because he was hot as sin and obviously enjoying my food, but Mr. Allen didn't need to know that.

The man blew out a breath. "Thank you. It might not have been him, but I'm glad you were vigilant. I'd love to have you cater our board meeting next month, by the way."

My heart danced. The more jobs on my calendar, the better. Didn't matter how overbooked I was, or how many late nights I spent cooking and prepping. This was my life—well, this and brewing my healing potions. I was happy to throw myself twenty-four-seven into cooking and catering. It brought me joy. And it meant I was too busy to think about how lonely I'd become.

"I'd be happy to, Mr. Allen." I reached out to shake his hand. "Just send me the details, and I'll put it on my schedule."

The man nodded, shook my hand and turned away from me. I slapped a hand over my mouth to hold back a laugh, because the man's pants had split clear down the back seam revealing a bright red pair of underwear.

Clearly he hadn't realized this. I was pretty sure I knew who was to blame for this wardrobe malfunction. And I must be just as bad as the demon, because I giggled to myself and never said a word, letting Mr. Allen walk all the way up to his house with his underwear showing.

CHAPTER 3

GLENDA

I thought about my upcoming catering jobs as I navigated the van over the twisted roads that led over the mountains, through the wards, and into the town of Accident. Most of my work was outside of the wards, in the human world of artfully decorated cupcakes and crust-less sandwiches, but the next two jobs were inside the wards and for non-human clients with some non-human culinary tastes.

Wednesday was a birthday party for one of the gnomes. Gronk was turning two-hundred years old, and this shindig was shaping up to be a sort of gnome bar mitzva. There were roughly eighty gnomes in Accident at any given time, most of them living in the underground tunnels they'd built to the east of the town. They weren't completely subterranean, though, and this party would thankfully be held somewhere I'd have access to electricity.

Next Saturday was the event I was most excited for. Everyone in Accident had been pitching in to help rebuild Dallas' compound after a rampaging fire-breathing T-rex burned most of it to the ground. It was a tragedy that had brought the two warring werewolf factions together, and so far that peace seemed to be holding up. It had been Cassie's idea to have a huge party to celebration the completion of the compound restoration, to hopefully continue the good-will between the two werewolf packs and the town. And what better way to make werewolves happy and thinking of peace-not-war, than filling their bellies with an amazing selection of roasted and smoked meats prepared by yours truly.

It had been a long day, and I knew I'd have several hours of unloading the van and cleaning up before I could yank off my shoes and my bra, and sprawl across my bed, but I still took a left turn once I hit Main Street, knowing it would save me time in the long run if I detoured and picked up a few essential things. The gnome party wasn't until Wednesday, but a few of their requested foods required a long marinade and pickling, as well as fermentation, and the sooner I got started on those, the better. So I drove to the edge of town and turned off the dirt fishing road that ran along Hop Mill Stream. About three miles out was a little grove and a section where the stream became a tiny pond that sparkled with light both from above and below.

I parked a respectful distance and watched where I walked, ringing a set of wind chimes and waiting at the edge of the grove. The water bubbled, and a naked woman rose from the depths, her blue-green hair fanned out behind her, her body elongated and inhumanly fluid.

"Glenda Perkins." She smiled, her voice like rain against summer leaves. "You are here for the *schallea?*"

"I am." I watched as she walked along the surface of the water, her feet becoming more solid as she stepped onto the mossy ground of the grove. "How are you doing Besellia? We missed you at the Koi festival this spring."

She waved behind her at the water, then bent down to

retrieve two bottles from behind a tree. I looked and saw two pairs of eyes staring at me from the edge of the pond.

"I gave birth in March. Twins. It was not easy, and they have kept me busy. I was sorry to miss the festival, though. Perhaps next year when they are older." She handed me the bottles and tilted her head toward the eyes with a fond smile. "Do not have children, Glenda Perkins. They drain the life out of you."

I laughed, knowing she was teasing. "Thanks for these. If you need anything, you know to call—or come get me."

She patted my arm, her hand cool and wet. "We owe you much more than these two bottles of *schallea*. If it hadn't been for you, Fennta would have died."

I felt myself flush. As easy as it was for me to accept praise and gratitude for my cooking, it wasn't so easy for me to do the same with my healing skills. Maybe because I felt it was my duty. I was a Perkins, a witch, and I was born with the responsibility to help the residents of Accident with my magical skills. There were no thanks necessary. Healing was my calling, a charge given to me at birth. Where Cassie had chafed at her duties, I'd always embraced mine. Not that I blamed Cassie. Her responsibilities were a hundred-fold what mine were, and she'd been thrust into a parental role at a young age, taking care of the six of us as well as herself when our mother had skipped town.

"I was glad to help Fennta. And if you ever need someone to watch a couple of young water sprites so you can head over to Pete's for a drink or two, you let me know."

She laughed. "I'll take you up on that once they're older. Right now, I'd be afraid they might drown you." There was a bubbling noise from the pond, and Besellia's head turned so fast I thought she'd get whiplash. "And now I must get back to these little minnows. Hope to see you soon, Glenda."

I echoed the sentiment and watched as she melted back

into the pond, the two sets of eyes vanishing with her. Shouldering the two heavy bottles, I took them to my car, stowed them in my trunk, and headed to the second stop of the evening.

Alberta and Shelby lived under a bridge, which was awesome for Alberta but less so for Shelby. The werewolf seemed to be adapting though—evidence of how much she truly loved the troll.

Personally I thought their tiny cottage under the bridge was adorable. It was way too small for all my kitchen gear, but as far as a living space went, it was really cute. The house reminded me of a child's play house, only taller because although Alberta was short for a female troll, she was still six foot two inches with the muscle to match. Shelby was six inches shorter with a lean strength, but with the two of them, I'm sure the little cottage made for some tight space.

Shelby answered the door at my knock. The werewolf was still sporting a short stylish hairdo that would require daily trimming to keep in shape, and she was wearing a super cute white swing dress dotted with a print of red cherries.

"Whoa! I want that dress," I told her.

She beamed, doing a little pirouette. "You like it? It was a gift from Alberta. She bought it at a shop on the other side of the wards."

Shelby said this with a sort of awe that I completely understood. The modern human world wasn't the threat for witches as it had been when my ancestor Temperance Perkins had founded the town, but it still was terrifying for many of the supernatural beings that called Accident their home. The wards kept them safe from harm, and any humans that ventured into town conveniently forgot about all the mermaids, shifters, vampires, and fae when they left. It meant everyone in Accident was free to look and be as they truly were.

For Alberta to cross the wards and purchase a dress in a human shop, she would need to use her troll glamour to appear human. It was a risk she'd taken for Shelby, but it wasn't a huge risk. Trolls were incredibly skilled at glamour, and the only threat to her would be if she somehow lost her connection with the magic-giving earth and lost her hold on the illusion. Although *that* catastrophe would probably only result in people running and screaming, not shooting her or trying to drown her. Modern times were kinder to the residents of our town, but they still felt safer inside our wards.

Most werewolves didn't believe that. They'd been raised with stories of being hunted and exterminated, of being tortured and imprisoned. Very few werewolves left the protective wards of Accident. Very few werewolves left the mountain they claimed as their territory. And of the few that did, most sweated through the whole experience, dashing back to the safety of their compound as soon as possible. I could count on one hand the number of werewolves who felt comfortable spending several days in the outside world, which was strange since they looked and seemed just like humans until they shifted into their wolf form.

"I need Alberta to do my shopping for me," I teased. "She's got great taste in clothing. It looks amazing on you."

She flushed again, smoothing her hands down the front of the dress. "Thanks. Can I help you with something? Do you want to come in and have tea or coffee?"

"Actually I needed to pick up something from Alberta. Some herbs and spices she had for me?"

The troll was obviously not home. Their cottage was so tiny that I would have seen her from the doorway had she been.

"Oh my. She's out and won't be back until late." Shelby turned. "I think they're in the kitchen, though. Hang on a sec."

I waited while she walked the ten feet to the kitchenette and looked through a box on the counter.

"Here they are!" The werewolf lifted a handful of paper bags triumphantly in her hands. "Four bags, right? Two have leafy things, and the other two have…seeds?"

I chuckled. "Yes, seeds. They're some unusual herbs and spices for the gnome party on Wednesday. Not the type of stuff that I'd have on hand, but I knew Alberta could find them."

She crossed the room and handed me the bags. "She's good at that sort of thing. Our garden is amazing, and she brings back all kinds of bark and berries and nuts from the woods. I don't know what half of things she cooks are, but I try a bite or two so I don't hurt her feelings. I know she does the same with the rabbits and deer I bring home."

I shook my head, thinking what an odd couple this pair were. But sometimes the two people you thought least likely to fall in love ended up head-over heels. I could tell Alberta and Shelby were happy and they made an adorable couple.

"Are you both coming Saturday?" Part of the peace treaty that my sister Sylvie had negotiated with the two werewolf clans involved allowing those who'd been exiled or who were living as lone wolves to join in on a monthly hunt, and to attend special events at either compound. This barbeque was supposed to be one of those events—the first where that part of the deal would be tested.

Shelby twisted her hands together. "I don't think so. It's supposed to be a happy event. I don't want my presence to create tension."

"My sisters and I will be there," I assured her. "You'll be safe and so will Alberta."

"I know. That's not it, though. It's bound to be uncomfortable for both of us as well as those in my former pack.

The looks, the snubs, the snide comments…I'm just not ready for it yet."

I understood, but someone would need to make the first step, and a barbeque would be a little easier event to transition than the full moon hunt.

"Will you think about it? Maybe just show up for a short time? I know it will be tough seeing your former pack mates and worrying about what sort of reception you'll get, but it's a step in the right direction."

Her mouth twisted into a grimace. "Okay. I'll talk to Alberta and maybe we'll just pop in for a moment or two. If Dallas and Clinton give me a cold shoulder, then I'm leaving. I love your cooking, Glenda, but even your smoked pork loin isn't worth people saying mean things about Alberta and me."

"Understood."

She was right. I'd talk to Cassie and Sylvie and see if they could somehow convince Dallas and Clinton to extend a public civil greeting to Shelby and Alberta. They didn't have to hug them or hang around all afternoon like besties, but if they welcomed the exiled wolf to the event, then their packs would at least know to keep their nasty comments to themselves.

Thanking Shelby, I said that I hoped to see them both at the party next Saturday, and headed for my car. I was driving back to town, lost in thought and musing over my upcoming events, as well as thinking of a sexy demon, when I noticed a car by the side of the road. It looked like someone had been changing a flat and gave up. The vehicle was lopsided, lowered down to the axle in the left front. I glanced in the rear view mirror as I drove past and slammed on the brakes, realizing there were a pair of boots sticking out from under the car.

There were humans who called Accident their home, and supernatural beings who wouldn't survive having the weight of a car fall on them. Fearing the worst, I dialed the firehouse and frantically dug through my trunk for my jack.

Pierre answered and I let out a relieved breath. I was within the wards that surrounded Accident, and dialing 911 might get me a human rescue squad. The moment the humans left town they'd forget all about whatever supernatural might be trapped under that car, but I still didn't want to take the chance that this would be the one time in centuries our wards failed us. Plus there was a good chance a human EMT wouldn't have any idea how to care for whoever was trapped under that car.

"Pierre! I'm out on Hollow Ridge, about a mile south of Beaverton Road. There's a car on top of someone."

The vampire shouted to someone else, then turned back to the phone. "A rollover?"

"No. Looks like he, or she, was changing a tire and the car came down on him. Or her." I found the jack and cradled my phone against my shoulder as I hauled the pieces out of my trunk.

"What kinda car?"

I could hear the sound of an engine starting in the background, and hoped they were leaving with or without Pierre.

"I don't know." I lugged the jack parts over to the car and eyed the front. "A Hyundai something or another. Silver with primer gray on the fender. I'm guessing it's a guy because the feet in boots look kinda big, but it could be a troll."

Oh no. There were other trolls that came and went from Accident, but my mind automatically went to Alberta. No. Shelby would be devastated if something happened to her mate, although I doubted getting squished by a car would be enough to kill a troll.

"Feet, not fins!" Pierre shouted to someone else. "We'll be right there, Glenda. Hang on."

I dropped the phone as he hung up and began to assemble

the jack as fast as possible. Then I reached under the car, half afraid of what I might feel but knowing I needed to position this jack under the frame of the car or risk it coming down a second time on whoever was under there. The metal was sticky with what I hoped was some kind of automotive fluid. Determined not to think of it as blood, I shoved the jack under the frame and began the incredibly difficult task of trying to hoist the car up off the ground.

Why didn't I own one of those nice hydraulic jacks instead of this cheap piece of crap that had come with my car? It was taking every bit of strength to budge this stupid Hyundai, and my jack looked like a flimsy piece of tin foil trying to hold up a…well, a really heavy car. At least Cassie had taught me how to do this when I'd turned sixteen and gotten my license, insisting that I be able to change my own tire if I got caught out somewhere with a crappy cell signal. We might be witches, but none of us could magic a spare onto a car. Unfortunately.

Terrified that my jack wouldn't hold, I stopped when the car was a mere ten inches off the ground, and swallowed back my fear enough to crawl partway under and see who this unfortunate motorist was.

When I saw Stanley, I nearly wept, partly because I hated seeing him like this, and partly because as a werewolf, his chances of living through such a horrible accident were pretty much guaranteed.

I'd grown rather fond of Accident's second exiled lone wolf and made a point of chatting with him every time I went into Petunia's Auto Repair, Bait, and Beer shop. I was there to get beer, because I didn't fish, and thankfully my car hadn't needed repair during the last year. Stanley was a werewolf of few words, but get him talking about cars or fishing, and he'd go on for hours. I might not fish, but I certainly was very interested in fish that could be smoked, fried, baked, broiled, or stewed, so Stanley and I had become friendly. He'd brought me a nice trout last week, and in return I'd dropped a batch of blackberry muffins off at Petunia's as a thank-you.

"Stanley. Oh, Stanley."

The werewolf shuddered and I tried not to gag as I saw his face better in the dimming sunlight. His body was strangely dented, crushed from the front of the car, but it looked like a particularly heavy part of the undercarriage had come down hard on his head. It was a flattened, bloody oval. A human never would have survived this. A witch never would have survived this. I wasn't sure a werewolf could. Crushed ribs, broken pelvis, internal bleeding, fractured jaw —all that would heal in a few days or weeks' time for a shifter. But I knew things like being blown into little bits did a werewolf in. It had to do with damage that was too catastrophic to heal before decay set in. Stanley was all in one piece, but it was his head that bothered me.

Nearly every werewolf in Accident had a concussion weekly, but I'd never seen one with half his skull caved in.

"Pull me out."

His voice was bubbly and soft, and I couldn't help but flinch.

"I think your spine is broken. And your head… It's probably not a good idea to drag you out by your feet. The medics will be here soon. Just hang on, Stanley."

"Don't wanna be under this car. Back'll be fine. Pull me out."

I cautiously eased my way out from under the car, figuring he'd know better than me what injuries a werewolf could heal from. With a grimace, I grabbed him by the heels of his work boots and pulled, not liking the way his body stretched out or the wet gasps he made as I slowly slid him out from under the car.

The expression of relief on the werewolf's face once he was free of the car told me I'd made the right choice. "Are you gonna be okay?" I asked, finally hearing the sirens coming up the road.

"Don't…know. Head. Can't think."

Ophelia and Pierre would know better than I how to position Stanley so his supernatural healing would work best. I felt so helpless, and I was the witch whose talents lay in healing. But my skills were more along the line of augmenting or speeding up the natural process. I could shorten the time it took a broken bone to knit, reduce the recovery period for the flu. I wish I could do more than create healing potions—my smoothies that did the job but always tasted so foul. I wished I could truly heal, just channel my power and repair any wound, eradicate cancer, make every part of someone's body whole and healthy with a wave of a hand and an incantation.

But I couldn't, so instead I held Stanley's hand and cried silent tears as I waited for the vehicles coming up the road.

Ophelia and Pierre jumped out of the ambulance with Ricky close behind. I stood back and let my sister and her vampire co-worker help Stanley while Ricky jotted down a bunch of notes on a pad of paper attached to a clipboard. He took my statement, then wandered over to the Hyundai while I hovered near Stanley, hoping for some good news.

"This your jack?" Ricky called.

I shot Stanley a concerned glance, then wandered over to him. "Yeah. That one there, I don't know where the one Stanley used was. I'm assuming he used one."

Ricky shrugged. "Might have just tried to pick the car up with one hand and change the tire with the other. I've done it before when I couldn't find my jack, or when half of it was missing."

I could totally see Ricky doing that, large round belly and

all, because he was a bear shifter. Not that werewolves were slackers when it came to strength, but they didn't quite have the muscle mass that bears did. Plus there was one other thing that made me doubt Stanley had been using the technique Ricky had suggested.

"He was under the car, flat on his back. I don't think he would have been in that position if he'd been holding the car up with one hand and turning lug nuts with the other."

Ricky's thick unibrow practically shot up to his hairline. "Why was he underneath the car if he was changin' a tire?"

I blinked in surprise, because I hadn't even thought of that. Yeah. Nothing Cassie had taught me about changing tires had involved scooting underneath the car with the tire off and the vehicle perched precariously on a cheap, comes-with-the-car jack.

Glancing over at where my sister and Pierre were working on Stanley, I hoped he'd be able to answer these questions.

Ricky grunted. "Found the jack. But what the acorns and walnuts is it doing way over here?"

I looked to see where he was headed and saw him pick up a hunk of metal from across the road. Now that was just as much of a mystery as what Stanley was doing under the car. I'd assumed the jack had broken, or the gears hadn't held the car in place, but if that was the case it would have been lying next to or under the car, not all the way across the road.

I glanced back at the Hyundai, but didn't see any signs of an explosion or something that might have propelled the jack so far away and allowed the car to drop down onto Stanley.

"Looks like it's okay," Ricky said. "Not sheared off, or any damage that might have caused it to drop the car."

That I didn't quite take as any sort of clue, given that I was skeptical that such a flimsy jack could reliably hold a car upright anyway. But why had Stanley been underneath? I never would have crawled under a car supported by my crappy factory jack if I hadn't been trying to save someone's life.

"He's stable," Ophelia announced. "I've got everything aligned, and relieved some of the cranial pressure. Glenda, do you have anything to speed his healing along?"

Now that I could do. I walked over to see Stanley on a stretcher, his back supported and bandages holding everything where it needed to be. His face still appeared a mess, but his eyes were alert as his gaze met mine. I gave him a smile, then went to the trunk of my car and pulled out a bag. Inside were half a dozen twenty-ounce drink containers, each containing a different potion. I chose the one I'd prepared for traumatic injuries, carefully brewed during the spring equinox, and passed it over to Ophelia. She flipped open the lid. A straw popped out, and she held it to Stanley's lips.

The werewolf shot me a piteous look.

"Drink it," I told him. "You'll be on your feet by tomorrow instead of laying in your bed for days or even weeks."

He did as I said, gagging and choking as he forced the smoothie down. I knew it probably tasted like old gym socks, cow poop, and ground beef that had sat in the summer sun for three days, but it was powerful stuff. Watching Stanley's aura, I saw it brighten, glowing with the greenish gold of spring's first leaves. That was when I knew he'd be okay.

Pierre and Ophelia stood, standing back a bit as they watched Stanley. He grunted, sweat breaking out on his forehead as he slowly moved his toes.

"Spine's healing first," my sister commented. "That means either the brain injury wasn't all that severe, or that Stanley didn't have any brain to injure."

The werewolf made a raspy noise that I realized was a

laugh. "Only need the brains for fishing and car repair," he quipped.

I felt the adrenaline drain from me, realizing he'd truly be okay. "You scared the heck out of me, Stanley. I'm glad I glanced in the rear view on the way by or I wouldn't have seen your feet sticking out from under the car."

"Thanks, Glenda." He gave me a faint smile. "For the healing potion, too. Although I hope I never have to drink anything like that ever again."

I laughed. "Just don't go crawling under cars supported by crappy factory jacks while you're changing a tire, okay?"

He frowned, looking puzzled. "Tire blew, but there was a leak. Was worried it was coolant and I'd overheat, so crawled under to check."

"And the jack gave way," Pierre finished the werewolf's sentence.

Stanley shook his head, wincing at the motion. "No. Jack was fine. Someone...I think someone kicked it out. I remember seeing a foot, and a shadow, then the car crashed down on top of me."

Ophelia looked over to me, one eyebrow raised in a silent question.

"Ricky *did* find the jack across the street," I told her. "I can't imagine how it would have gotten that far if it had broken."

"And it's not broken," Ricky confirmed, holding the jack up for Ophelia to see.

"If someone kicked it away..." Ophelia let her voice trail off, her eyes meeting mine.

I knew exactly what she meant. If it had been me kicking a jack away, it would have been right next to the car. Actually I doubted I'd have the muscle to kick a jack out from under the car it was supporting. No, that sort of thing would take supernatural strength, whether the perpetrator kicked it clear across the road, or flung it there after the fact.

Either way, I believed Stanley. And that meant at the very least we had an assault that had occurred in our little town, if not an attempted murder.

CHAPTER 4

GLENDA

It was dark by the time I left the accident site, and as I drove I couldn't help but think about Stanley. Ricky had made a call to Sheriff Oakes before they'd even loaded the werewolf into the ambulance, and Ophelia promised to update me tomorrow at our family dinner, but the memory of what Stanley had looked like when I'd crawled under the car haunted me the whole way home.

Had someone really tried to hurt him, maybe even kill him? Stanley used to pal around with Clinton and his friends, getting into bar fights and joining in drunken vandalism from when they were teens until just a few months ago, but I couldn't recall that he'd done anything that might get him singled out for revenge among the other townsfolk of Accident.

Anyone who met Stanley today would think he was just a chill werewolf who dug working on cars and fishing, but he'd gone through a wild phase the same as every other shifter. But I was pretty sure none of that would cause someone to drop a car on him. No, I was convinced the motive for tonight's attack came from the events surrounding Stanley's exile from not just one pack, but both of them.

Where Shelby's offense had been loving a troll, Stanley's had been what both packs considered treason. When Clinton had broken off a splinter faction from his father's pack—the result of which was nearly a war— Stanley had remained a supposedly loyal member of Dallas' group.

Unbeknownst to Dallas, Stanley was acting as a spy and secretly aligned with Clinton. It hardly seemed in keeping with his aw-shucks personality, but the werewolf had pulled it off until Clinton's group had gone too far and nearly gotten my sister Bronwyn killed.

Stanley had risked his life to do the right thing and help my sister, blowing his cover and getting himself exiled. We'd heard rumors of individuals in both packs who wanted him dead, but we'd granted Stanley asylum and protection since we were the witches who ran Accident. Dallas and Clinton had made it known to their followers that they didn't want to jeopardize their ability to live inside the wards by killing someone under our protection, which should have kept him safe. That didn't mean someone wasn't still willing to risk it all and kill Stanley. Emotions ran high among shifters, and with werewolves, loyalty to the pack was expected.

I resolved to put it all out of my mind until tomorrow. Ophelia would keep tabs on Stanley's recovery and what the local law enforcement was doing about his claims. I'd drop off another potion at the hospital to help speed things along in case my previous one hadn't been enough magic to get Stanley on his feet and back home. We'd all discuss the issue of who might want Stanley dead enough to defy their alpha. And I'd let Cassie know that this peace and the inclusion of the lone wolves would never work unless Dallas and Clinton made an effort to personally welcome both Shelby and Stanley at the barbeque on Saturday.

I made the turn down my street and stuffed my thoughts into the back of my mind. It had been a long day. I really wanted nothing more than to crawl into bed, but there was still work to be done. Pulling into my driveway, I headed inside and switched on the lights. Most people would find my house odd, but for me, it was perfect. When I'd bought it, the one-story house had two bedrooms and a jack-and-jill bath off the back. The front section held a living room to the right of the front door and a dining room to the left with a small kitchen in between the dining room and the wall for the smaller bedroom and bathroom.

I'd promptly knocked out all the interior walls except the one bedroom and the bathroom and converted the spare bedroom, living room, dining room, and kitchen into one enormous kitchen.

It's not like I'd ever had friends over or anything to require a sofa or any area to eat. If I wanted to watch TV, I did it from my bed. If I wanted to eat, I pulled a stool up to one of the long stainless-steel tables and ate.

Yep, I'd turned my house into one giant commercial kitchen. The little electric stove and fridge were gone, replaced with a walk-in I'd had custom built and a series of six ovens as well as an eight-burner gas stove. I had two mixers so huge that they had to be on the floor, plus several smaller ones. There was a giant butcher block, a marble-topped table complete with a cooling system for confections. Just walking into my house made tears come to my eyes and a warm feeling spread through my chest. I'd made this place my home. It might not be what anyone else would consider a reasonable place to live, but for me it was perfect.

There was a time when I'd had other hobbies. As a kid I'd played kickball, swam in the ponds and streams, and climbed up the rocky slopes of the mountains that bordered the north and west sides of what was Accident. Yes, I spent a lot of time in the kitchen, and I remember my Grandmother teaching me how to make pies and biscuits when I was so young I needed to stand on a chair to reach the counter.

In my teen years, I still enjoyed scrambling up the rocks in the mountains, but more and more of my time had been spent in the kitchen. By sixteen, I knew what I wanted to do for a living with as much certainty as how to make a smoothie that would heal burned flesh overnight.

Rock climbing was still fun, but I'd put that aside for a spatula and some high-quality saucepans. I'd barely made it to my high school graduation because by then I already had catering events scheduled pretty much every moment I wasn't in school. An all-consuming romance at the age of twenty had almost put the brakes on my obsession, but when that had gone up in flames, I'd found solace in the one thing that had always been there for me, the one thing that had never let me down, the one thing everyone loved me for—my cooking.

Putting the *schallea* in the fridge and the herbs and spices on the counter, I began the exhausting task of unloading all the trays and supplies from the Allen engagement party. When I was done, my normally clean and tidy kitchen was a mess of dirty pans, utensils, and serving platters. I eyed the chaos, wondering if I could get away with leaving it all until morning. But I knew I wouldn't be able to sleep soundly knowing this was all waiting for me, and no one likes to wake up to a stack of dishes with dried-on food, so I rolled up my sleeves and dug in.

By two in the morning I'd dried the last shiny, stainless steel serving tray and placed it neatly on the wire rack with the others. Done. And now it was time to relax.

I poured myself a big glass of shiraz, and headed for my bedroom, shedding my clothing as I went. A long hot shower and a glass of wine later and I was feeling mighty pleased with myself. It had been a good day, outside of Stanley being squashed by his car. I had a happy client who'd promised repeat business. I'd picked up the supplies I needed to get started on the delicacies for the gnome party. I had two events scheduled for next week that I was really excited for—two events that wouldn't take me outside of my beloved Accident. Plus, tomorrow was family dinner night and I was looking forward to seeing my sisters, their significant others, and the racoon that Bronwyn always brought and slipped food to out the kitchen door.

As I slid in between cool, soft sheets, I thought of the party and my mind kept returning to the demon. I didn't even know his name. I'd probably never see him again. But as I drifted off to sleep, I felt myself warm at the thought of his wicked sexy smile, and the naughty glint in his bright blue eyes.

CHAPTER 5

GLENDA

n spite of getting to bed fairly late, I was still up at
dawn, caffeinating the sleep out of my body and
thinking about what I should bring to family dinner tonight.
Munching on an extra scone from an order, I hauled the
book where I kept all my recipes out and settled in for a
leisurely morning.

My house is at the outskirts of town, on a quiet residen-
tial street where chain-link fences separate the miniscule
backyards. Most mornings I sit on my front porch and wave
to the neighbors whose jobs require they be up just as early
as me. This was Sunday, though, so I was on the back patio,
noting that Mr. and Mrs. Boogness, the goblins who lived
two houses down, were also sitting on their back patios,
bleary-eyed as they watched their son chase his new pet
possum around the yard.

Young goblins are adorable in the way that 1980s troll
dolls are adorable. I watched the kid play, then smiled over at
his parents, raising my cup of coffee in a salute to all of us up
early on a Sunday.

Hmmm. What should I bring to family dinner? Cassie

was always in charge of the main dish, which meant there was a comforting predictability about what we ate. Baked ziti. Meatloaf. Stew. Pot roast. Fried pork chops. Roast chicken. Spaghetti with meat sauce. Enchiladas. Every now and then my eldest sister would branch out and make something that we hadn't had every week growing up. Those were the Sundays where we usually ended up calling for pizza delivery. Just as I was the only one who'd been gifted with the magic of healing, I was the only one in our family who seemed to be able to cook.

There was no way Cassie would be awake this early, so I sent a quick text to Bronwyn, asking her if she knew what the plans were for a main dish tonight. Then I slipped a few sticky notes in to mark recipes that I thought I'd like to prepare—a white bean and prosciutto side dish that would be a good accompaniment for a variety of meals, and two cornbread recipes. One cornbread was sweet and moist, and the other was spicy with bits of minced jalapeño.

Setting my recipe book aside, I refreshed my coffee from the carafe, and grinned as I heard Brian Holter across the street fire up his abnormally loud lawn mower. No amount of complaining from neighbors made a difference in the routine of one of the few humans that lived in Accident. Every Sunday, Brian mowed, trimmed, edged, blew leaves or snow all at an ungodly hour of the morning. I never minded since I was awake anyway, but others were incensed by the loud noise just as the sun was coming up on a weekend.

Sylvie, my therapist sister, claimed it was Brian's way of asserting himself as a human surrounded by stronger, faster, and magically powerful supernatural beings. Personally, I think he did it because he was a jerk.

Bronwyn texted back that last she'd heard we were having pot roast, so I decided on sweet cornbread and headed inside, grabbing my carafe of coffee. Closing the door didn't completely block out the mowing noise from across the street, but I lost myself in cooking, not even noticing the sound after a few minutes.

Putting the cornbread in the oven, I got dressed and puttered around my house for the rest of the morning, oddly uneasy. My home had always been a sanctuary. I'd never minded my rather solitary lifestyle, immersing myself in cooking and finding great joy in both the magic of my healing smoothies and creating food, but today I felt strangely empty.

For once, I didn't just want to hang around my house until it was time to head to Cassie's, so instead I grabbed a few things from my fridge and headed to the hospital.

I was thrilled to see Stanley dressed and being helped into a wheelchair by a dryad nurse. He was pale and a little wobbly, but looked so much better than he had just twelve hours earlier. I handed him a box of honey pecan cookies and a to-go cup of my healing smoothie then asked how he was feeling.

"Better." He sniffed at the smoothie and grimaced.

"Drink it," I ordered. "I want you at work tomorrow like nothing happened. *And* at the barbeque on Saturday."

He sighed, flipping the lid and downing the potion with a shudder. When he was done, he wiped his mouth on his sleeve and handed the cup back to me. "Not sure I want to come Saturday, especially after what happened last night. Thinking I won't be welcome. Thinking I might end up dead."

I bristled at the thought. "Not on our watch. Cassie will be there. All of us will be there. We'll make sure you're safe—both you and Shelby. I'm asking you as a friend, Stanley. I'd like you to at least make a brief appearance. Exchange a few words with the non-werewolves, as well as with Clinton and Dallas, then eat something and leave if you want. It's important, not only to you and Shelby, but to anyone else who might end up being a lone wolf in Accident."

He opened the container of cookies and popped one in his mouth. "Okay, Glenda. But only because I trust you and your sisters to keep me safe."

The nurse smiled at me and I took over, guiding the wheelchair through the hallways. "You need a lift, Stanley? Who's taking you home?"

"Bart."

The one word sent a flood of emotion through me. Stanley and Bart had been best friends before Stanley's exile, and I knew they'd been meeting clandestinely to chat and go on a few fishing expeditions. This was big, though. Bart had always been nervous about being seen with Stanley after his exile. That he'd roll up to the hospital and give his friend a ride home, meant that the other werewolf had finally real- ized their friendship was more important than what anyone in his pack might say if they were seen together.

Of course, it helped that Dallas and Clinton had both agreed that lone wolves did not have to be shunned as part of their recent peace treaty, but this was still incredibly brave on Bart's behalf.

"You said last night that someone kicked the jack out from under your car," I mentioned once we were alone in the elevator.

Stanley nodded. "I made a statement to Sheriff Oakes. I'm not surprised, honestly. Been getting subtle threats at work and around town. Even had notes stuck on my car or in my door at home telling me to get out of town."

"Does Cassie know about this?" My voice trembled with anger at the thought that Stanley was being harassed, that he'd been attacked—all while under our protection.

"It's an ongoing thing," the werewolf waved a hand in the air. "No sense in bothering your sister about vague threats."

"It's not vague threats anymore, Stanley."

He nodded. "I know. But I'm not sure what anyone can do about it, even you Perkins witches. I'll show up at the barbeque because you asked, but after that, I'm gonna keep my head down and hope whoever dropped my car on me leaves me alone."

This had to stop. If someone was disregarding our town's laws as well as the werewolf alphas' peace treaty, then that someone needed to be brought to justice. As much faith as I had in Sheriff Oakes to get things done, the barbeque was Saturday. That event needed to go off smoothly, to set the tone for what the future held for both the werewolf packs as well as the other beings who lived within the wards of Accident. Our sheriff was a dryad, but even a dryad and head of our law enforcement community would welcome help from seven witches.

I wheeled Stanley through the lobby where a middle-aged male werewolf fidgeted. There was an old model Ford pick-up idling just outside the hospital doors.

"Bart." Stanley smiled at the other werewolf. "Thanks for giving me a lift. Sheriff Oakes said I won't get my car back for another day or two."

"Hope they put a new tire on it before they drop it off," Bart drawled. He looked up at me and nodded in recognition. "You gonna catch the guy that did this? Don't like anyone messing with my friend here."

"We will." I passed the wheelchair off to Bart and watched as the two werewolves headed through the hospital doors. Bart helped Stanley get settled in the truck, then came back in to return the wheelchair.

"Gonna stay with him a bit, just to keep an eye on him. Make sure he's doin' okay. Make sure he gets some food in him beyond this hospital stuff." Bart fixed me with a steady gaze. "It's what friends do. Don't care what others in the pack might say. Don't care if it makes me a target too. It's what friends do."

I watched him go back through the doors, climb into the driver's side of the truck, and head down the road. He was right. And for the first time in my adult life, I wished I had a friend like that, wished I had someone making sure I was doing okay, wished I had someone to come home to.

CHAPTER 6

GLENDA

I pulled up to Cassie's house early, eager to see my family and recapture that comfort, that sense of order and routine that had governed my life so far. But within the comfort of family dinner, I knew there would be some serious issues to discuss. The werewolves. Stanley. Shelby.

But those were conversations for later. I parked my van, got my bags from the back seat, and walked right on in the house. Early as I was, I wasn't the first one here. In fact, it looked like everyone had arrived early except for Babylon, who lived outside the wards of Accident, and had a habit of being fashionably late.

"I'm ready for some pot roast," I announced as I walked into the kitchen.

"Well, too bad because I changed my mind and we're having enchiladas instead." Cassie walked over to give me a kiss, and suddenly I was surrounded, six sisters all hugging and greeting me.

Well. Good thing cornbread went just as well with enchiladas as it did with pot roast, although I was wishing I'd made the spicy one with jalapeños rather than the sweet kind.

"Hi Glenda." Lucien shot me a friendly grin, and even though they looked nothing alike, his smile reminded me of another—one that was naughty and suggestive, one that had made my heart beat faster.

It might not be the right time to talk about Stanley and the werewolves, but it was definitely the right time to talk about that mysterious crossroads demon who'd haunted my dreams last night.

"So…" I tried to keep my voice casual as I pulled the warm cornbread from my insulated carrier and sat it on the counter. "I met a demon yesterday, and I've got questions."

The entire population of the kitchen froze for a brief second, then everyone spoke at once.

Cassie waved her hand to silence the crowd. "Who? What's his name? How did you meet him?"

I figured that probably summed up most everyone's questions, but I took a second to check the temperature of the cornbread before answering.

"I met him at the Allen engagement party but didn't get his name." I went on to tell them all about the party as well as the very sexy demon I'd encountered.

"Sounds hot," Adrienne announced.

"Sounds dangerous," Cassie countered.

Ophelia shrugged. "I'm not getting any warning vibes. I'll do a reading later to double check, but I say go for it."

"It's been too long since you've gone out, either on a date or with a friend," Sylvie said. "I respect that your magic and your career bring you great joy, but if this demon attracts you, then I agree with Ophelia. Go for it."

"Kinda hard to go for it when I don't know this demon's name, and I'm hardly likely to ever see him again," I drawled.

Bronwyn laughed. "Are you kidding? He's tasted your

food. He'll be back. You'll probably find him begging at your door tomorrow morning, hoping you'll toss him a muffin or a piece of that ginger cake."

"Mmm, ginger cake," Ophelia said. "That's my favorite."

"I'm thinking if shows up at your door, you should tell him to take a hike. Crossroads demons are bad news," Lucien warned me. "When you met him at the party, he didn't offer you a deal? Challenge you to a contest? Did he try to make you a bargain? To take your soul?"

"No. He was too busy eating to do any bargaining. Or even to make Mr. Allen's life miserable." I couldn't help a smug smile at that. "One bite of my food, and he was captivated. He tried all the different foods, parked himself right beside the buffet table. And there he stayed until the party ended, when he disappeared."

"Left fat and happy." Adrienne nodded. "I agree with Bronwyn. He'll show up within the next few days, wanting more of your *goodies*."

I flushed. "Hopefully the goodies he's interested in aren't just the kind I create in my kitchen."

"Well, I still think you're better off without him," Lucien told me.

"Not me." Eshu grinned. "Personally I like crossroads demons. They're fun."

Lucien gestured toward Eshu. "See? That's even more reason to stay away from this guy."

I doubted I'd see the demon again anyway, but I did take note of both opinions. And I turned to the other two males in the room. "Thoughts?"

Hadur shrugged. "I've not had much dealings with crossroads demons."

"I have," Nash chimed in. "I see them when they're collecting a soul I'm releasing. They're tricky, but they abide by the rules of their contracts. Of course, it seems their contracts are often worded to allow them lots of flexibility in interpretation."

"Well, I don't have a contract or a bargain with this guy. I just wondered if I should give him a tentative green light in case I see him again."

"Do you think you'll see him again?" Cassie shot me a worried look.

I shrugged. "Maybe. He really liked that ginger cake. He might show up and ask me for the recipe." I pursed my lips in thought. "What kind of bargain could I strike for that? Do you think I can get a demon soul for a recipe?"

Adrienne snorted. "Demons don't have souls."

Hadur scowled. "Yes we do. And I don't think anyone would give up their soul for a recipe."

"You clearly haven't had Glenda's ginger cake," Cassie told him. "It's totally worth selling your soul. Totally."

"It is," Lucien agreed.

"Heaven pales in comparison," Eshu added. "And I should know because I've been there. Glenda's ginger cake is one of the seven wonders of the world as far as I'm concerned."

I blushed, but still felt a surge of pride. Of everything in my life, I was most proud of my cooking. Which was odd given that I could create magical potions that accelerated healing.

"Well, hopefully the cornbread passes everyone's scrutiny." I laughed and slid the pan onto the stovetop to stay warm while the enchiladas cooked.

Babylon showed up with two cases of beer and a container of guacamole that she said her neighbor had made. We all ate chips with salsa, queso, and guac, drank beer and laughed, reminiscing about our childhood. Even the demons chimed in with stories of hell. By the time we all sat down for enchiladas, black beans, and my cornbread, I was feeling a happy buzz that had nothing to do with the beer Babylon had brought.

My family. As much as I loved my solitude and my kitchen, these Sundays with my sisters were the highlight of my week. And the addition of four men to our weekly family event only made it better. I enjoyed watching them interact with everyone, as if they'd been part of our family forever. I loved seeing Cassie and Lucien's public displays of affection, Bronwyn and Hadur exchanging adoring glances, Ophelia and Nash's easy rapport, and the way Sylvie and Eshu bantered back and forth.

I wanted that. I want all that. It shocked me a little, because before yesterday I'd never thought twice about having another in my life. A long-term boyfriend. Love. Companionship. Maybe even marriage and kids. Suddenly that appealed to me and it scared me because I truly didn't think that was at all feasible given the way I'd organized my life to date.

Somehow Hadur's raccoon ended up inside the house, eating scraps as well as tortilla chips from Bronwyn's hand. After dinner we all cleared the table, the guys shooing us out of the kitchen to relax and drink another beer while they washed up.

Before I could turn the conversation, Ophelia took charge and steered the topic where I had wanted it to go.

"Stanley's doing well, by the way. He was released from the hospital this morning."

I nodded. "I know. I stopped by and wheeled him downstairs. Bart was there to drive him home. He's staying there a bit just to make sure he's okay."

"I was so pissed off that I nearly set my house on fire when I heard," Cassie said. "Didn't help that Sheriff Oakes told me this morning that Petunia found evidence of tampering with Stanley's car."

Bronwyn caught her breath at that. One of the were-wolves had tampered with her truck and she'd gone off a cliff and nearly died. The parallels were disturbing.

"Does Sheriff Oakes think it's the same werewolf that messed with Bronwyn's truck?" I asked.

Cassie shook her head. "I doubt it. That werewolf knows he's banished from Accident the next time he pulls something like that. No, the sheriff and I think this is someone who has a personal grudge against Stanley—or feels his betrayal of Dallas or Clinton was a crime worthy of severe injury or death."

"He's gotten threats," I told the others. "The sort of threats that flat out say he needs to leave town or else."

"He's under our protection." Ophelia's eyes narrowed in anger. "Whoever is doing this is disrespecting our authority."

"Respect our authority!" Babylon said in a weird voice that made me think she was quoting something or someone. Adrienne laughed, but the rest of us looked at her and Babylon cringed. "Sorry. I couldn't help it."

"He's not just dissing us," Adrienne added. "He's going directly against the treaty that Sylvie brokered, against the treaty both alphas agreed to."

"So a renegade," Sylvie mused. "I'm thinking maybe one of the traditionalists Dallas spoke about that might not be happy about the treaty."

"Whoever he is, he's determined," Bronwyn added. "Sheriff Oakes brought by that jack for me to look at, and someone had taken a rasp to it. They wanted it to fail, but clearly followed just in case it didn't."

I caught my breath. "We've got to stop whoever this is. Stanley did the right thing in blowing the whistle on what happened with Bronwyn's car. We need to protect him and send a strong message that this kind of thing won't be tolerated in Accident."

"I'm thinking we need to work this at both ends." Cassie took a swig of her beer and leaned forward. "Sheriff Oakes is investigating. I'm putting some additional protections around Stanley. Bronwyn is making an amulet. Ophelia is going to do a divination at midnight tonight. Sylvie is creating a luck charm. Adrienne is sending some of her animal friends to both watch over Stanley and to spy on the packs."

I exchanged a knowing glance with Babylon. My youngest sister sighed and shrugged.

"What should Babylon and I do?" I asked.

Cassie blinked. "Umm. Maybe you could make a healing potion, just in case? And Babylon can…be ready in case we need an army of undead?"

Babylon and I exchanged another glance. This was such bullshit. True, my healing powers weren't much when it came to offensive magic, but I had a brain and could still work to investigate stuff at my end. Babylon too. I hated how she was always shuffled off to the side, her magic too icky for any of us to really think of using.

Instead I just nodded, realizing that Cassie was probably right. I didn't have the sort of magic to take care of this situation. I was in the right place at the right time last night and was able to help Stanley out. I'd prepare potions and do my best to deal with any issue my sisters couldn't prevent. I guess that was my role in all this.

"There is one more thing." I looked over at Cassie. "This peace might work out between Dallas and Clinton, but it's not going to deliver what was negotiated for the lone wolves unless those alphas make it a point of welcoming Stanley and Shelby."

Sylvie nodded. "I agree. I think there are many were-wolves who think the alphas, especially Dallas, didn't truly mean that part of the negotiation. That might be why Stanley is being attacked."

"Stanley has agreed to come to the barbeque," I said. "Even with the risk. I told him we'd protect him, but we need to get Dallas and Clinton to agree to personally welcome both Stanley and Shelby. Alberta, too. I know it will be a hard pill for them to swallow, but just by making a point of greeting them and spending a few moments talking to them, it will prove to both packs that all the terms of the peace treaty are to be abided by."

Cassie let out a long breath and exchanged a glance with Sylvie. "We'll work on getting the alphas to agree to that. Ophelia, can you do a divination to give us an idea of what we might encounter at the barbeque? Bronwyn, can you put together some non-violence charms for us to spread around? Adrienne, can you have woodland creatures and insects at the ready in case we need to subdue a werewolf? Glenda, I'd like you to have a few of your smoothies available in case someone is injured. And work your magic in your food so everyone is too busy enjoying the party to bother with any feud they may have."

I opened my mouth to protest that my magic had nothing to do with my food, only to pause. An image flickered from my memories of a sexy demon, so busy eating my food that he completely forgot about torturing Mr. Allen.

"I'll do it," I promised.

"What about me?" Babylon asked.

Cassie frowned. "Um, just be ready to...I don't know, frighten the werewolves into submission with an army of undead somethings?"

"What kind of dead should I raise? There might not be any fresh animal carcasses nearby. How about the werewolf graveyard? That would freak them out. Or maybe I should bring my own corpses to raise?"

Cassie squirmed. "No, that's okay. We probably won't need to raise any dead, but just be ready, okay?"

Babylon slumped, and I felt a bit sorry for her. Yeah, animated dead were really freaky, but it wasn't her fault she'd been gifted with a magic that made the rest of us uneasy.

"Bring some dead rabbits," I whispered to her. The werewolves would either chase them, or run away, depending on how fresh they smelled.

My youngest sister smiled at me and lifted her hand for a fist bump. "Got it. You cook and make those horrible smoothies, and I'll take care of the zombie bunnies."

CHAPTER 7

GLENDA

I made a detour on my way home, unable to shake my persistent worry that something else might happen to Stanley. Seeing Bart's car in the driveway was a relief, but I still parked and headed up to the door, just to make sure all was okay. This was one of the times that it sucked to be a witch with only one magical ability. Healing was great, but when it came to defending someone, protecting someone, or fighting, I was pretty useless.

Bart answered the door and ushered me in. I immediately saw Stanley stretched out on the recliner, a plate of what looked like chicken tenders on his lap and a television remote in his hand. His face paled as he saw me.

"Please tell me you're not here to make me drink more of that stuff," he pleaded.

"If I had any more with me, I'd definitely make you drink it." I looked him over. "Although you look pretty good, Stanley. I'd never know you'd been flattened by a car just last night."

"It's my fried catfish," Bart said. "Makes everything better."

I eyed what the contents of Stanley's plate with grudging respect. Fried food wasn't really my thing, but they did smell darned good.

"Any word from Sheriff Oakes?" I asked the werewolf.

Stanley and Bart exchanged uneasy glances. "No," Stanley replied. "It's okay. I didn't have much to tell him. Might have even imagined the whole thing. My jack probably just broke or something."

I blinked at shock about the sudden change in his story. Even without any magical spell, I could tell he was lying.

"Stanley, I heard that your car had been tampered with, and that there were rasp marks on your jack. You said you saw someone. It wasn't your imagination."

Stanley shook his head. "I'm gonna ask Sheriff Oakes to drop it. I was working on the car earlier, so it was probably my fault about the leak. And the jack."

"What happened? Did you receive a threat? Was there another attack?" I demanded.

"Told him he needs to let it go," Bart told me.

I stared at him, wondering how the werewolf so upset over his friend's injuries and determined to get to the bottom of this had changed his mind in less than twenty-four hours.

Bart must have seen my thoughts in my expression because he sighed and ran a hand through his bushy brown hair. "I know, I know. After I got Stanley home though we got to talking and I got to thinking. Now's not the time to be stirring up things in the packs. Give it a few months and this will all start to blow over. If Stanley lies low, then whoever this is will probably leave him alone. He pushes it, starts insisting on being accepted as a lone wolf, starts attending functions and hunting with the packs, and it will only get worse."

I couldn't believe I was hearing this. "But you're still coming to the barbeque, aren't you?" I asked Stanley.

He shook his head, his eyes not meeting mine. "It's not wise, Glenda. Best to let the two packs patch things up without my putting a burr under the saddle."

I knelt down beside the recliner. "Stanley, you didn't do anything that would have triggered this attack on you. You've stayed away from Heartbreak Mountain. You haven't participated in any pack events. Since you were exiled, the only thing you've done is get a job at Petunia's and go back and forth from work and your house in town. If someone found your presence in Accident, your very existence, reason enough to attack you, then what makes you think laying low is going to prevent it from happening again? This person clearly wants you dead."

Stanley stiffened and Bart came around me to put a hand on his shoulder. "I'll be here. Two sets of eyes, you know. Pair of us will make sure nothing happens."

Stanley made a low grumbling noise. "Gonna follow me back and forth to work, Bart? Stay here every night? That's gonna piss off the pack more than me going to a durned barbeque or having Sheriff Oakes investigate."

"It's gonna be okay," Bart assured him.

The other werewolf shrugged off Bart's hand. "It's not gonna be okay. And if I'm going to wind up dead, I'd rather the law makes sure Dallas punishes the killer. Or the witches punish the killer."

Bart sighed and held up his hands. "Okay, but I'm telling you right now that if you wind up dead, Dallas and the witches ain't gonna be able to punish anyone, 'cause I'm gonna take that wolf out with my own claws."

A smile flickered across Stanley's face. "I'll go the barbeque, but I don't want you there. I don't want to risk you losing your place in the pack, or having others target you."

Bart frowned. "You think I can't be at the barbeque and pretend I'm shunning you?"

Stanley chuckled. "That's exactly what I'm thinking. One of us is going to say something or act friendly, and you're going to be a target as well. Can't do nothing about what's happening to me, but I'll be danged if I do anything to cause you to lose your pack."

There was a low, long growl that came from Bart's throat, and Stanley reached up to pat his arm. "Knock it off. You're the one who said to lay low and that things will get better soon enough. It's too late for me to erase that target on my back, but no sense in having one on yours as well. Stay away from the barbeque, and we'll meet up for fishing Sunday morning. I'll even bring the beer."

Bart shook his head and scowled. "Okay. But only 'cause you're bringing beer next Sunday."

Stanley lowered his hand, then he took a deep breath and looked over at me. "There's a few things I need to tell you if I'm gonna go ahead with this. Once I started feelin' better, I started remembering more. That foot I saw? Had a boot on. It was a sort of hiking boot with a red stain about the size of a dime on the toe."

"Blood?" I grimaced, not wanting to make an assumption here. Werewolves were hunters and it wouldn't be all that unusual for one of them to have blood on their boots.

"Not blood. Wasn't colored like blood," Stanley said. "It was like paint or something. Not soaking into the leather like blood would, but sitting on top. Thick and bright red."

I considered that for a moment, not sure what to make of the fact that the assailant had red paint on their boot. Werewolves tended toward neutral colors in their home décor, but one of them might have been painting a child's toy, or something else. Maybe it wasn't a werewolf that had attacked Stanley. We'd all been assuming so, but perhaps one of the other supernaturals in town had a grudge about an auto repair, or the length of his grass or something like that.

"A boot," I mused. "That rules out a handful of residents like satyrs, centaurs, and minotaur who don't have feet to wear hiking boots."

"It was definitely a werewolf," Stanley told me. "I caught his scent."

"Then you must know who it was." I stood, excited at the prospect. One phone call to Sheriff Oakes, and another to Cassie, and they'd be on their way up to the mountain to arrest the assailant.

"I don't." Stanley looked embarrassed at the confession. "It all happened too fast, and he was covering up."

"He was what?" I had a sudden vision of a werewolf in paint-stained hiking boots and a burka.

"Covering up," Bart interjected. "It's when we use something to hide our scent. Werewolves got good noses, so we can't totally hide it, but it works short term when the wind is in your favor."

"Like mud? Or coyote urine?" I asked.

Both werewolves made a face.

"No wolf is gonna put coyote piss on himself," Stanley told me. "It was Drakkar."

I was so confused. "Drakar? Isn't that Swedish for dragon? You make yourselves smell like dragons?"

Bart chuckled. "Now *that* would be funny. Can you imagine showing up to a hunt smelling like a dragon? Half the pack would piss themselves running away."

Stanley waved a hand at his friend. "That's not what I mean. Drakkar. The men's cologne. Caught a faint scent of werewolf, and I'm surprised I managed that. The guy had enough Drakkar on him to ruin my sense of smell for an hour. Well, for an hour if I hadn't had a car dropped on top of me."

This was something I'd never known about werewolves. "You all do this? I mean, does every werewolf have a bottle of

Drakkar in his house just in case he wants to drop a car on someone and not be recognized by scent?"

"Nah. Mostly we use it when we're dogging some other wolf's lady, or stealing a chicken." Bart grinned. "Females used to use Opium, but sometimes they use Drakkar too if they want a werewolf to think a male is stealing his chickens."

"So you're not sure this was a male werewolf?" I asked. "It could have been a female with paint-stained boots wearing a bottle of Drakkar?"

Stanley shrugged. "Might have been. I thought it was male, but didn't get enough of the werewolf scent to tell and females are just as physically strong as males."

I frowned, thinking of something else. "Someone in the pack has to know who this was. I can't imagine a werewolf coming home reeking of cologne and no one noticing it. Heck, that much Drakkar and I'll bet the entire compound smelled him or her coming from a mile away."

"That's if he or she went home," Bart pointed out. "Lots of us go out for a hunt and don't come back 'til morning. That's what I'm supposed to be doing right now."

I eyed him in disbelief. "And the scent would wear off in that time?"

"Shower a couple times. Swim in the swamp. Roll in mud. Kill a deer and wear it's skin around for a few hours." Stanley nodded knowingly. "There's lots of ways to get the scent off. Plus if you shift a few times, it helps it wear off fast."

Crap. Still, this information was better than nothing at all. I wasn't a detective, but Sheriff Oakes and Cassie could certainly get to the bottom of this. Maybe someone at the compound had heard another werewolf spouting off about Stanley. And it couldn't be too difficult to figure out which werewolves were out "hunting" on the night in question.

"Thanks guys." I shook Bart's hand and patted Stanley on

the shoulder. "I'll be back tomorrow morning with another smoothie for you. Just to make sure you can get through the work day without collapsing. Let Petunia know you might need a light work day or two. He's discreet, and he can come up with an excuse to let you take a long lunch and get off work early if you need."

Stanley smiled. I let Bart escort me the twenty feet to the door and cast a careful eye around as I walked to my car. The night seemed peaceful with cicadas singing in the moonless night, but I couldn't help but feel a shiver run up my spine as I unlocked my car and climbed inside.

It felt like someone was nearby, like someone was watching.

CHAPTER 8

GLENDA

I was up with the sun, once again relaxing on my back porch this time with a giant mug of coffee and a thick slab of buttered sourdough toast. My next door neighbor was also an early riser this morning and he saluted me with his own cup of coffee, the faint light of the sunrise reflecting in his fiery eyes.

"Morning, Kane," I called out. "Come join me. I've got a warm loaf of sourdough and a pot of fresh ground, fair trade Ethiopian."

He hesitated, then shook his head with a reluctant smile. "I've got to head up north to drop off a commission and a few pieces at the gallery. Next time?"

"Of course. Be safe."

The ifrit was always safe. Anyone catching sight of his unusual eyes thought they were some weird techno contacts the artist wore as part of his edgy, punk image. Kane used to need an intermediary to deliver his artwork to the human world, but the last decade he'd been more comfortable venturing out on his own. Emboldened by the non-threat-ening reaction to his appearance, he'd even taken to attending gallery events and as a result, demand was increasing for his art.

Who knew burned wood sculpture could be so lucrative?

I sat alone on my porch, watching as the sun fully emerged over the horizon, hearing the town come to life as people started about their day. Kane loaded artwork into his bright red SUV and waved as he drove off. I finished my coffee and the last bite of my toast and headed inside, feeling oddly empty. I had plenty to do today. I'd stayed up late last night making potions that might be useful if there were injuries at the werewolf barbeque, but the rest of this week would be devoted to non-magical preparations.

First though, I needed to go visit Stanley.

Putting a Thermos of healing smoothie into my giant purse, I headed out. The werewolf was just about to leave for work when I arrived. Bart's car was no longer in the driveway.

"He left before sunrise," Stanley said, noting my expression. "Trust me, I had to practically fight him to get him to go. I didn't want anyone at the compound suspecting he'd been here with me. Bart likes being part of the pack. I'd feel horrible if he got kicked out on my behalf. Besides, I'm fine. Whoever attacked me probably figures I'm either dead or in the hospital."

I handed him the Thermos and hid a smile at his grimace. "Drink. Go to work. Make sure you tell Petunia you might need an extra break or two."

He took the Thermos and hesitated. With a stern look from me, he unscrewed the cap and drank it down.

"Don't taste any better the third time. Sakes alive Glenda, how can you cook food the angels would fight over but your magic potions taste so darned horrible?"

I laughed. "Trust me, if I could figure out how to make them taste better and still heal, I would. Sometimes you need to suffer, you know? There's a price for everything in this world, and downing a horrible-tasting potion is the price for healing magic it seems."

Stanley shuddered. "Wish it didn't taste like butt and paint and rotted cabbage though."

I took the empty Thermos from him. "Is Bart coming by tonight?"

The werewolf regarded the ground intently. "Don't know. I hope so, but I don't want him getting in trouble."

"If not, then you need to let me know," I told him. "Cassie's going to make sure you've got wards around your property and Bronwyn's working on an amulet for you. We've got your house covered, but maybe a couple of Sheriff Oakes's deputies can keep watch for tonight, or Cassie and Lucien can swing by to check on you."

Stanley shifted his weight, his nose wrinkling as he glanced up at me. "Hate for everyone to go to all that bother. I'm a werewolf. I'm fine."

"You were squashed by a car less than a day and a half ago," I retorted. "You may feel fine, but I don't think you're as strong as you normally are. Let us help, Stanley. You're part of our community. This is what we witches do for residents of Accident. And it's what we do for friends."

He nodded, his smile warm. "Thanks, Glenda. I really appreciate it, you know. I'm thankful that you saw me there under the car, and that you've been helping me with your magic. When I was exiled from the pack, I felt so alone, but you, and Sylvie, and your sisters have been good friends to me. I hadn't expected that. It's good to know I've got friends."

"You most definitely have friends."

I let myself out, making sure I locked the door as I left. In spite of the huge to-do list I had waiting for me at home, I made a detour to the fire department. The doors were open revealing the big ladder truck in one bay and the ambulance in the other. The smaller response vehicle had been pulled out and Skip was there, topless with a pair of Daisy Dukes, washing the truck. The fact that he was a half giant meant it was easy for him to clean the roof. It also meant that every time he leaned forward, his jean shorts rode up and I got a nice view of the lower half of his hairy butt hanging out.

I waved, Skip returning the gesture with a soapy sponge; then I headed inside to see my sister Ophelia sitting on a wooden folding chair, reading a book. She set it aside as I approached, rising to give me a hug.

"What's up?"

I glanced at the cover of the book, intrigued that she was reading a biography of Benjamin Franklin.

"Wondering if you had a moment to do a divination for me?" I asked.

"New moon." She grimaced. "And Mercury retrograde. I couldn't even do the scrying that Cassie wanted me to do. The only person I could perform a fully accurate divination for right now would be Eshu."

I smiled thinking about the demon, or god of chaos, or whatever my sister Sylvie's boyfriend was. "How about a less than accurate divination?"

"About you and that crossroads demon?" Ophelia wiggled her eyebrows and I felt myself blush.

"No, although if he comes up, I'd love any information you can give me on him. What I really want to know about is Stanley—especially if you can give me any insight into who might have attacked him as well as if he's in danger of another attack in the near future."

Ophelia nodded. "Come into the kitchen and I'll see what I can do."

I followed her back through the firehouse, accepting a dark, hot cup of coffee from Brandy who was finishing up with the breakfast dishes. She took one look at Ophelia and smiled, excusing herself to give us privacy. Given my sister's work schedule, her co-workers were used to the firehouse kitchen being home to Tarot cards and crystal balls in addition to coffee cups and pots of spaghetti.

I sat and waited for her to pull out a bag of runes or cards, but instead Ophelia sat a small mirror on the table between us.

"Sit and drink your coffee while I concentrate."

"What, no Ouiji board?" I teased.

She lifted one eyebrow. "And wait here all day while the planchet spells everything out one agonizing letter at a time? Ain't nobody got time for that."

I chuckled, then fell silent, watching and sipping the dark sludge in my mug as my sister worked her magic.

"A false sense of peace then danger," Ophelia whispered. "Red. Not blood, but red…paint? It smells familiar but I can't quite place it. Obnoxious ladies-night-at-the-disco cologne. Rocks. Something that I think might be chocolate. Meat spilling off a plate as it falls to the ground."

"*That's* a crime," I told her.

"Hush," she scolded. "A choice. A crossroads…no, more of a fork in the road. One path requires trust at great risk. That path drops from sight a few feet in. I can't tell if it goes off a cliff, or just slopes out of sight. The other path is straight, steady, and familiar, but the destination ahead is shrouded in mist."

That made no sense. The crossroads might have referred to the demon I met Saturday, but Ophelia's fork-in-the-road prophecy didn't seem to mesh with that interpretation. And I had no idea what any of this had to do with Stanley. The red paint, the cologne, yes, but the rest?

"Can you tell when the danger occurs?" I asked, leaning forward to look into the mirror which seemed like just a plain old mirror to my eyes.

She shook her head. "No, although the plate seemed to be falling into the grass, so maybe a picnic? Or the werewolf barbeque? Or Stanley grilling in his own backyard?" Ophelia sat back with a sigh. "I'm sorry, Glenda. The only other thing I'm getting is a vision of a big huge truck and trailer. It's fancy. I don't know what the heck that has to do with Stanley or even you, but it makes me happy."

I snorted. "A fancy new truck and trailer would make anyone happy. Maybe I win the lottery and replace my catering van? Or you guys raise enough for that new ambulance you all wanted?"

She smiled. "Or Stanley is the one who wins the lottery and heads to the Ford dealership, then decides to get a camper and tour the U.S. as a nomadic werewolf? No idea."

I stood and came around the table to give her a hug. "Thanks, Ophelia. I owe you one."

She squeezed me tight. "You owe me nothing. Well, except for some of those chocolate walnut cookies that Nash likes so much."

"Done." I made a mental note to bake cookies this weekend after the barbeque. I could give them to Ophelia at Sunday's family dinner.

Then I left, waving once more to Skip as I headed to my car. It was already late morning, and I had a gazillion things to do to prep for my catering jobs this week.

GLENDA

Once home I threw on an apron and got to work. There was the *schallea* to check on, adding the fruit puree that would make it especially appealing to the gnomes. I also needed to start pickling the turnips and marinating the slugs in the special herbs and spices I'd gotten from Alberta.

Ugh. Slugs. It wasn't the first time I'd made food for a client that I never wanted to eat. Catering jobs where a customer had completely different ideas of what constituted a delicious meal were always a gamble. I couldn't judge if I was getting it right or not and had to blindly rely on research, recipes, luck, and skill. Not magic, because although my magic potions healed, they tasted horrible no matter who drank them and I'd always been worried that combining my magic with my cooking would result in something inedible.

Oddly the excitement I normally would feel over a busy day in the kitchen wasn't there today. My career was rewarding. It was my life, my passion, the thing that put a spark in my heart and got me happily out of bed each morning. But today that spark just wasn't there. The thought of spending all day prepping and cooking seemed unusually depressing, and I felt an urge to…I don't know. I looked over at my cell phone wanting to call Adrienne or Sylvie, but it was Monday and I knew they were both busy with their jobs.

I was lonely. I lived alone. I worked alone. I had no friends beyond what I would call friendly acquaintances. Other than a few quick visits here and there like my trip to the firehouse this morning, I didn't see my sisters much beyond our family dinner. That had never been a problem before. In fact, that's exactly how I'd structured my life, how I wanted my days to be. I'd always enjoyed filling up my time with my work and peaceful solitude, but today it all felt…bleak.

I took a deep breath and ran my hands through my hair. Time to end the mopey pity-party and get to work. If I was feeling lonely then there was no one to blame but myself. I'd get all my prep-work done for the events, make the scones that Hollister had requested for some guests he had staying over tonight, then if I was still feeling blue, maybe I'd walk downtown and see what was going on. Dinner at the diner surrounded by others might help, or perhaps a trip out to Pete's for a beer, even though there wasn't much action Monday nights at the bar.

I pulled the turnips from the storage bin and began washing them when my doorbell rang.

Who the heck could it be? My sisters would have walked right in, and as I'd just been sulking about, I didn't have many friends that would come to call on a Monday. The bell rang again, so I put down the turnips and went to open it.

There was a demon was on my porch—the demon from the Allen engagement party. For a second I stared at him in confusion since I'd expected never to see him again. I mean, he did leave without even saying "goodbye". Or "thank you for the food".

"May I come in?"

My manners instinctively took over and I stood back, waving my arm for him to enter.

"Thank you."

His smile was charming, and it sent all sorts of happy tingles through my body. Once inside, he looked around, nodding in approval. I'm not sure if he was admiring the fact that my living and dining room had been converted into one giant kitchen, or if he had a thing for stainless steel.

"I don't really have anywhere for you to sit," I apologized. "One of these stools, maybe? Can I get you some tea? Coffee? Lemonade?"

He looked intrigued. "Lemonade?"

I got to work, because lemonade was better freshly made. As I squeezed lemons and pulled the simple syrup out of the fridge, I watched the demon. He looked oddly comfortable on the decidedly uncomfortable kitchen stool, and was taking in the ovens, refrigerators, and giant Hobart mixer.

"What's your name? I didn't get it at the party Saturday." I asked.

"Xavier." That slow sexy smile curled up the corners of his lips again. "And you are Glenda Ann Perkins, witch of the town of Accident."

Yes, it was mildly creepy that he knew my name, but I wasn't terribly surprised since he'd probably found that out to track down where I lived. Of more interest was his name.

"Xavier? That's not a demon name. That's a name that should belong to a sexy somewhat-evil twin brother on a daytime soap."

He shrugged. "I go by many names. I've had thousands over the last hundred years alone. Right now I go by Xavier, so that's what you may call me."

I barely restrained an eye-roll at that. "And I will grant you the supreme honor of calling me Glenda." I placed his lemonade in front of him and took a sip from my own. "Now, Xavier, to what do I owe this unexpected visit?"

He lifted the glass to his lips, his eyes widening at the taste of the lemonade. "This is quite good."

I waved a hand in false humility. "I use a specific lemon variety then throw in a little lavender, and my simple syrup is a bit different."

Because I wanted to show off, I pulled some dried apricot and dark chocolate cookies from a container and put them on a little plate, sitting them on the counter between us. Was he here just to eat? It wouldn't be the first time I'd lured a man in with my culinary skills, but those past relationships had failed spectacularly. Having a man who loved your cooking more than he loved you was a road that led straight to heartbreak.

"So why are you here?" *Please don't say my food. Please don't say my food.*

I watched as he ate a cookie, thinking that the expression on his face was pretty close to what a guy looks like when he shoots a load. Conflicting emotions raged through me—pride and a giddy happiness that he loved my cooking, and a worried sorrow that he wouldn't love me nearly as much.

But what did I care if some crossroads demon loved me or not? I'd just met him two days ago, and I was too busy for love.

"What do I need to do to get that ginger cake recipe?" His eyes were full of heat and promise and sin, but my heart sank. Of course that's what he wanted. I should have known.

"Trade me your soul," I teased. He was a crossroads demon, after all. I assumed this was the sort of thing he said to the humans who called upon him wanting wealth, or love, or fame.

"If I had a soul it would be yours." He smiled. "Perhaps there is something else you would like in exchange?"

Wealth, love, fame? But instead of pledging my soul to him in return, I'd be handing over a three-by-five recipe card?

"You can buy a cake, but not the recipe," I told him, thinking that he probably couldn't replicate it even if I did sell it to him. It seemed ridiculous that he'd tracked me down just to know what went into my cake. Yes, it was a darned good cake, but I wasn't quite so vain about my cooking that I'd think a demon would be willing to offer me more than just money for it.

But maybe the cake was an excuse and he was here to see me? I wiped that thought right out of my mind, because as confident as I was in my cooking, I was less than confident about my attractiveness. He was probably in town to see Lucien about some hellish matter and had stopped by hoping for lunch and a slice of cake.

"Who said anything about money?" The demon's eyes glowed, his smile downright sinful as his gaze focused on my mouth. The heat coming off him was delicious and his aura shifted, the swirls of orange growing brighter and countered by a deep violet.

I never gave away my recipes. Never. But something about this demon tempted me. Actually a whole heck of a lot about this demon tempted me. Plenty of boyfriends had loved my cooking more than me, but I'd never had anyone seriously offer to exchange sex for food—or a recipe. Figuring I'd play along with this, I turned on whatever sex appeal I might have and leaned forward onto the counter— which pushed my boobs together and upward.

"What exactly are you proposing?" I asked.

He eyed my breasts and wiggled his eyebrows. "How about one night where I make all your dreams come true."

"You'll do all the dishes, my taxes, *and* get me the catering job for the next inaugural ball?" I fanned myself. "Wow. You demons really do know what a woman wants."

He scowled, but I saw a hint of amusement in his eyes. "I was thinking more along the lines of my slowly removing your clothes, spreading you across your bed, then tasting every inch of you."

The demon went on to describe in incredible detail all the X-rated things he was going to do to me. I'm not a prude, but I was pretty sure my face was bright red by the time he finished. I'll admit, it did sound like something I would enjoy, and I did hesitate a few moments before answering him, just to make sure I'd fully considered his proposition.

But ultimately, I decided my ginger cake recipe was worth far more than one night of mind-blowing sex.

"Think I'll pass on that," I told him. "But if you'd like to stay and help me while I cook as well as wash the dishes, I might let you lick the spoon."

Something sparked in his eyes. "Can I lick other things as well?"

I smirked, thinking how shocked he'd be if he tried to lick the bowl I used to marinate the slugs. Although maybe demons liked slugs? The demons I knew seemed to have fairly human food preferences, but perhaps that was because we'd never offered them slugs.

"Maybe," I replied as I reached in a drawer and pulled out an apron. "Here. Put this on and go wash your hands."

"I need to clean my hands before I wash dishes?"

"Absolutely. Cleanliness is next to godliness—or satanliness, in your case. You might need to hand me a bowl or utensil before you do any washing. And I'm thinking you might make a good turnip stirrer. Are you a good turnip stirrer?"

He followed me, a bemused expression on his face.

"Turnips? I'm intrigued to find out what magic you're working that involves turnips."

"No magic, just food for a birthday party I'm catering on Wednesday."

I surveyed my ingredients. Vinegar. Sugar. Dill. Salt. Chilis. Some sliced beet to give them a pink color and an earthy flavor that I knew gnomes loved.

"You're preparing a dish with turnips for a birthday party?"

"Gnomes," I said, thinking that would explain it all.

It didn't.

"You're cooking gnomes and turnips?"

I rolled my eyes. "It's a gnome birthday party. Pickled turnips are one of the dishes on the menu."

The look of revulsion on his face was hysterical. And kinda adorable. I patted him on the shoulder and got out the saucepan, then walked over to the sink to add water.

"You're catering a party for *gnomes*?"

Putting the saucepan on the stove, I added my ingredients to the water, and turned it on high. "Last week I did a merfolk party. The week before that a centaur party. It's Accident. I need to be just as good at pickled turnips, sashimi, and oat-molasses bites, as Beef Wellington, Smith Island cake, and key lime pie."

He washed his hands and put on the ridiculously lacy apron as I peeled the turnips. Since I was already working on those, I asked him to dice some onions and prepare the marinade, then slice the slugs and add them to the bowl. Watching his face as he handled giant slugs made me laugh.

"Not quite what you expected, huh?"

He laughed, and the sound went right through me, making me catch my breath and press my thighs together.

"Not at all. I'd hoped for ginger cake, pie, or maybe even a smoked brisket."

I bit back a smile. "Well, I will be making sour cherry pie tomorrow, because in spite of their unusual taste in food, gnomes *do* love a sour cherry pie."

"I'll happily sample that." He smiled and for a second I forgot what I was doing.

"And brisket…I'll be making that for the barbeque Saturday. Werewolves love meat, so I'm cooking a lot of meat."

"Do *you* love meat?"

There was a whole lot of innuendo in that question. Once again I felt myself blush as I bent over and stirred the turnips with more force than necessary. "Only if it's well prepared."

"Noted." There was a moment of silence, and I felt the tension stretch out to the breaking point before he spoke again. "So what do we do when the turnips and slugs are done? Can I suggest something?"

I contemplated that for a moment, then chickened out. "No, you cannot. I've got a lot of prep work to do today for Wednesday's catering job. We'll cook today, but if you come back to help me tomorrow, I'll feed you lunch."

"What about I feed *you* lunch?" he asked.

I laughed. "Can you cook? I mean, you're doing a good job marinating those slugs over there, but what's your idea of lunch? Bologna on white bread with mayo?"

The smirk he sent my way was one-hundred-percent sexy. "Oh, I definitely can cook. Let's say we have a little bet. A contest. Tomorrow we'll both make a lunch dish. Whoever makes the best gets whatever they desire."

My heart skipped a beat, then I thought of my conversation yesterday at Cassie's. Lucien had warned me against bargains, contracts, bets, or contests with a crossroads demon. But I couldn't help feel a surge of competitive instinct at his suggestion. I'd win. I knew I'd win. No one was as skilled at cooking as I was.

But there was a little voice inside me that screamed caution.

"You need to specify what you will get if you win," I told him. "Because I'm not giving you my soul."

"How about your body?"

I sucked in a breath. Even with his flirting I'd expected he would ask for either my soul or my recipe for the ginger cake, not sex. I wanted to say "yes" to that bet. I wanted to say "yes" to him, but I was scared to admit that I wanted this demon. I'd just met him. I didn't know him. The logical, cautious me urged an answer of "no", but the thrill that ran through me at his suggestion, made me want to do something completely unconventional.

"Sure." I kept my voice casual, even shrugged as I pulled a container of flour out of the cabinet. "Why not? Come back tomorrow and we'll have a lunch-time battle of the chefs. Right now I'm too busy to think about lunch or even what I'm going to ask for when I kick your ass. So get your mind in gear, because we've got more cooking and a ton of dishes ahead of us."

"What else do we have to do?" He scrunched up his nose. "Please tell me I don't need to cut up more slugs."

"No, you need to make the sauce." I laughed at his horrified expression. "It's not that bad." I handed him the bag of herbs and spices that Alberta had given me. "Grind these up together with that mortar and pestle. Make them as fine as you can. Add them to a cup of chicken stock and a quarter cup of wine, then stick it all in the fridge."

He did as I instructed, whistling cheerfully in the background as I worked on my dough. We chatted about movies, music, our favorite crêpes. He finished before I did, then slid the bowl of sauce into the fridge before coming over to me.

"Bread?" He leaned over my shoulder and I resisted the urge to shift back just an inch so I'd be touching him.

"Yep. Gnomes love a good hearty bread. This recipe is based on a Russian black bread. A little sweeter but with the same thick, chewy texture and crumbly crust."

"And that?" He pointed to the ingredients I had on another table.

"Sour cherry pie. If you're a good boy, I'll make you cinnamon pinwheels with the leftover dough."

I felt him edge closer, felt the brush of his chest against my back. His arms came around either side of me to cage me in against the edge of the stainless steel table. "What if I'm a bad boy?"

"Then you might get a whole lot more than cinnamon pinwheels."

I felt my heart stutter, heat rising in my cheeks as I said it. This sort of banter wasn't anything I'd ever done before. Of all the Perkins sisters, I was the one least likely to naughty-talk, the one least likely to indulge in a one-night stand with a stranger. This was so out of character for me, but it felt right. I hoped he was a bad boy, because if he made a move, I wasn't going to say "no". Heaven help me, I never wanted to jump anyone as much as this demon.

I set my dough aside to rise, worked on the pastry for the pies, then showed Xavier how to use the cherry-pitter, leaving him to it as I checked on my bread dough and made the pinwheels.

When he was done that, I had him slice the cherries, and pulled the pinwheels out of the oven. Then I directed Xavier to put the cherries in one of the bowls chilling in the small refrigerator. Xavier removed the bowl from the fridge, hesitating a second. I bit back a smile, knowing what he saw.

"How in the world could there possibly be leftover ginger cake?" he wondered. "I'm sure I polished the rest of it off at the party—unless you were holding back a spare."

"I always make an extra one or two." I saw his questioning glance. "And yes, you can have some."

He cut a huge slice, making appreciative noises as he ate. "What's in the icing?" he asked. "I can't quite figure it out from the taste."

I smiled. "That, my dear demon, is a secret."

"Family recipe?"

"No, my personal recipe."

He finished the huge slab of the ginger cake, then pulled one of the still-hot pinwheels off the baking sheet.

"It's nothing big," I told him, suddenly shy. "Just leftover pastry dough, butter, and some cinnamon and sugar. My grandmother showed me how to make them when I was five and wanted to help her make pies. Ever since then I can't throw the dough away. I always make pinwheels and think of her."

My voice went soft as I remembered those days—my childhood before Grandma died, before Mom took off and left Cassie to raise us all. I didn't even have to close my eyes to see Grandma's hands with the fine bones and the network of brown spots. Her skin was smooth and cool, her hair in a long silver braid. When she laughed, it came up from deep inside her belly, shaking her entire body with joy. In many ways I missed her more than I'd missed my own mother.

Xavier took a bite, chewed thoughtfully, and nodded as he swallowed. "These are wonderful."

He stepped into me, holding out the remaining bit of pinwheel for me to eat. I leaned forward to take it and he brushed his thumb across my upper lip.

"It's more than food," he whispered. "There's history and love in these. These creations of yours…they're magic."

If he tasted my real magic he wouldn't think that at all.

"There's no magic in my cooking." I couldn't step back, couldn't look away from his amazing blue eyes. "I make healing potions, but they taste terrible. My magic makes them taste bad. I think it's a trade-off. There's always a price to magic, you know."

"There *is* magic in your cooking," he insisted. "Not healing magic, but something else."

"What?" I whispered, my gaze going to his lips.

"Joy. Community. Love."

His lips met mine, and I swear for a moment, the world stopped spinning. It wasn't one of those desperate, hungry kisses, but soft and full of promise. His tongue teased mine, and as he pulled away he nipped my bottom lip. It was over far too fast and I wanted more—I wanted so much more.

"I'm going to win tomorrow. And then I'm going to do a whole lot more than kiss you."

He left, and for minutes afterward, I just stood there in my kitchen unable to move. When I finally turned away from the door, I saw that he hadn't done the dishes.

"Darned demons." I headed for the sink, but there was a smile on my face and a skip in my step. I really didn't care about the dishes. What I cared about was tomorrow. Would he really be back? Could he actually cook, or was I going to have to choke down a bologna sandwich?

I hoped he could cook. And pride aside, I hoped he won.

CHAPTER 10

XAVIER

It took every bit of my willpower to walk out of that witch's home. I'd had many humans in my life, I'd enjoyed bodies, collected souls, given pleasure with one hand and torment with the other. But never in my incredibly long existence had I ever felt this magnetic pull toward someone. Never had I felt such peace and calm as in her kitchen, helping her cook. There wasn't just magic in her food, it was in *her*. It was in every motion she made, every word she spoke, every breath she took. With the act of creating food, she spun a spell of contentment and happiness over the entire house, painting it with vibrant colors and channeling all that into the delicious concoctions she made.

Glenda. Named, no doubt, after the good witch from that Oz movie I'd watched years ago. She *was* a good witch, and I was experiencing very conflicting emotions about that. The old crossroads demon in me wanted to corrupt her, to sleep with her and leverage her pride to secure her soul. The demon that I barely recognized as me wanted to curl up with her on a soft bed and spend the rest of my life watching her as she fashioned delicious foods with a wave of her hands.

I had work to do. There were humans ready to make deals. There were souls who needed to be collected, contracts that were reaching their conclusion. But I desperately wanted to go back there. I'd get as much done as I could tonight, then I'd return to her house tomorrow.

And then I might never leave.

CHAPTER 11

GLENDA

I'll admit that I was a little surprised to see Xavier at my door the next morning.

Yesterday had been a dream—a very happy dream that I hadn't wanted to end. But I didn't have the best luck when it came to romance, so I fully expected to never see the demon again. I'd never been so happy to be wrong.

"So, what are we doing today? Besides me winning our lunch bet and us spending the afternoon in bed." He clapped his hands together and strode into my house as if he belonged there. "Are we going to cook more gnome food? Human food? Martian food?"

I chuckled, shutting the front door and following him. "I've got no idea what Martians eat, but I'm pretty sure if I knew, I'd make the best feast they'd ever had."

Something sparked in his blue eyes—something I wasn't sure I liked.

"We're finishing the slugs today, and cooking the bread," I told him.

"So the menu for the gnome birthday party is slugs,

pickled turnips, bread, and sour cherry pie?" He counted them off on his fingers.

"It's more basic than most of my other parties," I agreed. "I also need to get going on the smoked meats for the big werewolf event this Saturday. I've got brisket, trout, and pork loin that all need to be dry rubbed and put in the smoker."

"Brisket?" he asked, that odd gleam back in his eyes.

I nodded.

He opened his mouth as if he were about to say something, then shook his head, a sheepish grin curling up the corners of his gorgeous lips. "Never mind. Let's get cooking. What can I do to help?"

We finished the sauce for the slugs and put them in to bake. We laughed over taste testing the turnips, debated the proper amount of vanilla to add to a custard, and prepared four different varieties of barbeque sauce for the werewolf party on Saturday.

Finally it was noon, and I felt my heart skip a beat as I realized there was no delaying our little contest. Not that I wanted to delay our contest, but the butterflies in my stomach meant I was absolutely not hungry at all. For food, that is.

"So…how does this contest work?" I asked a bit breathlessly. "It's lunch time. Should we both use the same ingredients, or are we free to use anything in the kitchen? What do you want to eat?"

He shrugged. "Anything except slugs?"

I laughed. "You sure? We could sample them once they come out of the oven."

"No way." He shuddered. "How about sandwiches? We can use anything we find in the kitchen, and we've got thirty minutes to put it together."

I grinned. Sandwiches. I could totally win this. I'd beat

the pants off the guy. Well, I hoped I'd beat the pants off the guy, because that would make victory all the sweeter.

"You're on." I bent to pull the panini press out from a lower cabinet while Xavier began pulling ingredients out of the fridge. I deliberately didn't look, not wanting to be influenced by what he was about to make. Hmmm. What to do, what to do? Turkey? Ham? Roast beef? Or veggie?

In the end I went with a chicken pesto with roasted red peppers and a layer of spinach on ciabatta. Xavier had been whipping something up in the food processor, and I had a little time, so I made a side of pineapple drizzled with honey as my imagination went wild with guesses about what he might be making that required a food processor.

"So what should I ask for when I win this challenge?" I asked him, not quite teasing. Of course I'd win. I always won when it came to food. Always.

"Anything you want."

I shivered at the suggestion in his voice. "And you said you wanted sex?"

His head lowered as he sliced his sandwich. "Maybe I want your soul as well as your body."

My hand froze over the pineapple. "Well, that's not going to happen."

He laughed. "I thought you were confident that you'd win? That there was no doubt at all in your mind that you'd beat a demon at making sandwiches."

I shivered again, but this time for a different reason. Of course I'd win. I always won. There was no way some crossroads demon was going to beat me at something I'd devoted my entire life to. No way.

And yet...

"I'm not wagering my soul over a sandwich. Pick something else."

"Scared?"

There was an odd note to his voice that I didn't like.

"Of course not, but you're not getting my soul if you win. Or my ginger cake recipe." It was a sad state of affairs when I was giving equal value to both my soul and my ginger cake recipe.

I looked over to see him pouting. It was so adorable, so sexy, that all my misgivings over the "I want your soul" thing vanished. My shoulders relaxed, and I shot him a quick smile.

"Can't have my soul. But you absolutely can have my body."

Crap. I'd said that? How embarrassing.

"Hmm, I think I want that more than your soul."

My breath caught at his response, and a mixture of giddy delight and relief flooded me. He wanted me. And that was one thing I'd be more than willing to give if the unbelievable happened and I actually lost.

We both sat across from each other on the tall stools, sliding plates across the table. I looked down and blinked in surprise to see what he'd made. I'd expected meat and a load of hot sauce between two pieces of bread, but instead I was looking at an open-faced vegan sandwich with endive, alfalfa sprouts, tomato, avocado, and hummus.

Hummus. That's what he'd been doing with the food processor. He'd made hummus from scratch. I swiped my finger across the edge of the sandwich and tasted, making an involuntary "mmm" noise as the flavors hit my tongue.

"Ras El Hanout," I murmured, instantly recognizing the spice blend.

He nodded. "I spent a century in what is now Morocco."

"I love Moroccan food." Had he known that? How could he have known that? For all my baking and traditional American cuisine, I adored the flavors of northern Africa and the near east. Suddenly my panini seemed pale and bland in comparison.

"Take a bite," he urged, his voice pure temptation.

I did as he said, and made appreciative noises as I chewed. This sandwich clearly should have been one of the seven deadly sins. For once in my entire life, I was about to lose a cooking contest. And I wasn't all that sad about it, even though my pride was a bit bruised.

He took a bite of mine. Then another. Then another. "This is amazing," he said with his mouth full. "Is this chicken grilled? Roasted?"

I wiped a smear of hummus off my lip. "Roasted. There's a farm on the other side of the wards that raises organic, free-range chicken. They're not traditional meat birds, so they take a while to mature and they have a lot of dark meat, but they're full of flavor. I think the farmer might add some saffron into their feed because the meat color and flavor is really unique."

We eyed each other for a moment, chewing.

"I hate to admit this, but I think you may have won." He slid the plate over to me. "Here. Try a bite. But don't eat it all because I want the rest of it."

We swapped sandwiches, and as soon as I tasted the one I'd made, I knew what he meant. The perfectly cooked, flavorful chicken, the pesto I'd whipped together, the fresh vegetables I'd gotten from a roadside stand, the red pepper I'd roasted myself and stored in olive oil…it was an amazing combination and the crunch of the ciabatta bread wrapped it all up in a delicious package.

"Mine's good, but yours is better," he admitted, taking a second bite of his sandwich and passing it over to me as he snatched the panini back.

I wasn't sure. Maybe it was because I really adored Moroccan food, but I truly thought they were equal, or that his was slightly better. But I couldn't imagine a demon would ever lie when there was no reason for him to do so. I couldn't imagine a demon lying to *lose* a contest. He must be telling the truth. And I'd come to realize over the last two days that Xavier knew what he was talking about when it came to food.

Maybe I wanted him to win so I'd need to give him what he wanted. It would give me an excuse to do what I'd wanted to do from the moment I saw him without all the angst and hand-wringing over how it wasn't like me to jump into the sack with a man, let alone a demon, that I'd just met.

"Yours is really good," I told him. "The hummus is amazing. It's a great combination of veggies, too. The crunch, the smooth spicy flavor of the hummus, the thick hearty bread, the creamy avocado—it's incredibly delicious."

He finished off the panini and slid off his stool. "Yours is better. Besides, you made the bread I used, so my sandwich wasn't entirely my creation. I'm not nearly as skilled at baking as you are. If it had been up to me, that sandwich would have been on Wonder Bread."

I burst out laughing. "I doubt that. I'm sure you would have found a decent bakery, or have made a nice country-style whole grain white. Anyone can make that. No one goes to the trouble of making their own hummus only to put it on Wonder Bread."

Xavier walked around the end of the long table and came to stand beside me. "You won our wager, witch. What should your prize be? What do you desire?"

My heart locked in my chest. It was him I desired. All I had to do was say the word. That kiss last night had been so far from chaste. I'd wanted him then, and here was my chance. If he'd won our little contest, I would have been in his arms without one word of protest.

But now it was me who had to make the move. I was the

one who had to tell him that I wanted him. He watched me, desire in his eyes as he waited for me to just say it.

"I...I want...a Mugnaini wood-fired pizza oven."

I kinda did. They were ridiculously expensive, and I'd never been able to justify it. Okay, actually I chickened out. I just couldn't admit that I wanted to have sex with Xavier. Maybe if I had a couple of glasses of wine I could, but not sober with him so close, watching me so intently.

"A pizza oven." His lips twitched and he reached down to pinch my chin. "Is that what you call it? A pizza oven?"

I sucked in a breath. "Not just any pizza oven. Wood-fired. Mugnaini."

"Mmm." He leaned forward and brushed his lips against mine. "I'll certainly do my best. Mugnaini wood-fired pizza oven, coming right up."

We kissed, my hands snaking up under his shirt as he unbuttoned mine. His hands were warm against my skin, his mouth teasing down my neck and shoulders. I felt my bra unsnap, and he gripped the lacy cup with his teeth, easing it down to release my breasts.

Everything became a blur of sensation as he kissed, licked, nibbled, and felt his way over my body. My pants slid down my legs, and I quickly unsnapped his, pushing them down to join mine on the floor. He was ready. I was ready. I was soooo ready. Grabbing his arm, I tried to maneuver him toward the bedroom, but he resisted.

In a blink I was up on top of the stainless steel table, dishes, bowls, and utensils sliding off to crash and clatter on the floor. Before I could protest, his head dove between my legs and all coherent thought fled my mind. He licked and sucked, bringing me to the very edge but not letting me climax.

"Damn it, Xavier," I choked out. My hands scrabbled for something to grab on the smooth table as my body tensed once more. Finally I reached forward to grip his shoulders, digging my short nails into his skin.

This time he let me fly, and the orgasm shuddered through me. My back arched off the table, but he held me in place with his hands on my rear. As I floated back to earth I started to giggle. My dishes were smashed on the floor. I was naked and sprawled across one of my tables. I didn't care. I didn't care that I'd need to clean up the floor and sanitize the table. I felt like every nerve in my body had risen to the surface of my skin. Everything tingled.

And I wanted to do it again.

Xavier eased back, brushing his hands down my sides and planting a kiss on my stomach. Pulling my hands from his back, he slid off the table and helped me to sit up. I should have been embarrassed. I was buck naked on a stainless steel table, looking at an equally naked demon. And the table was…messy. Looking down at the broken plates, the splattered food, the smudged and somewhat sticky table, I started to laugh. This wasn't something I ever imagined myself doing. It felt amazing. And I was about to do something else I never thought I'd do—ask this demon, someone I barely knew, to spend the night.

"Did that pizza oven meet your exacting standards?" Xavier grinned.

"Mugnaini wood-fired pizza oven level of awesomeness." I took a deep breath and went on, before my courage deserted me. "I know you're busy and you've got things you probably need to do, and I'm busy too with the gnome party tomorrow and…would you stay here? With me? It's okay if you can't. I mean, I understand. Maybe I'll see you around sometime."

He silenced my babbling with a quick kiss. "Yes."

"Yes?" I squeaked. "Yes, you'll see me around sometime?"

His smile was far too sweet and tender for a demon. "Yes,

I'll spend the night. I hope you actually have a bedroom, because as fun as this table was, I don't think it would be all that comfortable to sleep on."

"I have a bedroom," I assured him. Then I took his hand and led him to bed, with all that mess behind us. It could wait until morning. Everything could wait until morning.

CHAPTER 12

GLENDA

I woke up next to a naked demon.

He'd stayed through the night. And judging from the soft cadence of his breathing, I got the impression he wasn't going to be waking up for quite a while yet. Not everyone was up at the crack of dawn like I was. It didn't bother me one bit. In fact, I really didn't want to wake him, so instead I just stared at him as the faint peach glow of the sunrise began to make its way across my bedroom floor.

The sheets had tangled around his waist, leaving his upper body and legs exposed. I drank in the view, admiring the curve of muscles, the dusting of light hair, the way his chest rose and fell with each breath. I wanted so badly to reach out and touch him, to trace my finger along his sculpted arms. But there was something I wanted to do more.

Carefully easing my way out of bed, I tip-toed into the bathroom, brushing my teeth before making my way through the bedroom once more and into the kitchen where I tied an apron around my naked body and got to work. The sun had broken free from the horizon when Xavier stumbled from the bedroom, his hair still sleep-tossed, a towel wrapped around his waist, his face clean-shaven.

"Something smells amazing." He walked over and wrapped his arms around my waist, kissing me on the neck.

"Baked French toast casserole with crème fraiche and fresh berries. Oh, and bacon, because nobody seems to eat breakfast anymore without a large serving of meat." I scooted said meat around the pan with a pair of tongs and reveled in the feel of his skin against mine. From the hard-on poking me in the ass, he was reveling in the feel as well.

"I meant *you* smell amazing." He sniffed my neck, then nipped his way down to my shoulder. "Like sex and toothpaste and powdered sugar."

Heat rolled in one long wave down my body. The baked French toast could wait. The bacon could wait. But by the time we got done doing the mattress limbo, the puffy soufflé-like pastry would have fallen and become tough and chewy, and the bacon would be cold with congealed grease. As much as I wanted yet another round of sex with Xavier, I couldn't allow such a magnificent breakfast to be spoiled.

And honestly, I barely had enough time to enjoy a relaxing breakfast before I loaded up my van and got going. If this demon wanted more than one night, we'd have other opportunities for making love. Like maybe tomorrow, the day after the gnome party and two days before the werewolf barbeque. Maybe he'd accompany me to the barbeque. I'd love to introduce him to my sisters. I'd love to have him there by my side.

But first, breakfast.

"You turn the bacon," I told him, turning in his arms to hand him the tongs. The motion rubbed my naked butt along his erection, and my new position put it in just the right spot.

Ugh. Soufflé. Why couldn't I just have opened a box of grocery store donuts?

I reluctantly moved away from him. "I'm going to check on the French toast."

He made an appreciative noise as I bent over to peek into the oven, and I laughed, realizing that I was naked and my apron didn't exactly go all the way around my body.

"Mind that bacon," I scolded. "I don't want it to burn." Crispy, but not too crispy was how I liked it, and that required a lot of attention.

"I can watch both the bacon and your ass." He grumbled, although he did turn back to the stove.

"You overcook that bacon and I won't let you have any brisket at the barbeque," I told him. *Was* I taking him to the barbeque? Would he want to go? Would he stick around that long, or take off with some excuse about how this would never work out?

"I make a mean brisket myself." He shot me a naughty glance before looking down at the bacon. "If I don't get any of yours then you don't get any of mine."

I really wanted some of his, and I didn't just mean his brisket either, but I could never resist a challenge.

"Bet mine's better than yours."

He chuckled. "Your brisket? Or your ass? Because your ass is definitely better than mine. Your brisket most definitely isn't."

Oh, this demon was going to get the smackdown of his life.

"Gonna put your money where your mouth is, buster? We'll let the werewolf alphas judge, because no one knows meat like a werewolf. Dallas, Clinton, and Tink also in the unlikely case there's a tie."

"Deal." His smile was downright naughty. "You win, and you get whatever you want. I win and I get whatever *I* want."

I pulled a bottle out of the fridge and shut the door with my hip. "Anything? Anything I want?"

He nodded. "Anything. Your wish will be my command."

He bowed and I took the bacon tongs from his hand as he rose, giving him the bottle instead.

"Then it's a deal. Brisket wars begin tonight, and the winner will be decided Saturday at the barbeque. Now, pop this champagne. I've got fresh squeezed juice over on the table if you want mimosas, or we can drink them separately."

The "table" wasn't exactly an actual dining room table since I had no such room or piece of furniture. Instead I'd converted one of my stainless steel tables into a makeshift dining spot with a tablecloth, fancy disposable plates and utensils, and a pretty glass candelabra—all courtesy of my catering business. Thankfully the serving dishes were rather pretty since eating on paper plates, no matter how sturdy, didn't seem particularly romantic.

Note to self: buy dishes and silverware if this lasts more than a few days. Maybe even invest in an actual dining room set.

Why was I so pessimistic? We'd had an amazing time together the last two days. The sex had been mind-blowing. There was nothing in his words or actions to lead me to believe this was just a brief fling for him. I really needed to stop expecting the worst and focus on the positive for once. I needed to dump the baggage of my past horrible relationships and start this one fresh.

The loud pop of the champagne cork broke me out of my reverie.

I blotted the grease off the bacon as I took each slice from the pan, then neatly layered it onto a dish. Xavier was pouring the champagne, and I smiled at him as I sat the plate of bacon on the table. Then removing the French toast casserole out of the oven, I carried it over and carefully sat the baking dish into an ornate metal stand. Two cups of coffee followed, and we were ready.

Xavier came around the table to pull out the stool for me. In an impulsive gesture that mirrored my new positive attitude, I took off the apron and sat down for breakfast naked as the day I was born.

He laughed and whipped off his towel, tossing it across the room as he circled the table to take his seat. Our eyes met and he picked up his glass of champagne.

"To wood-fired pizza ovens."

I grinned. "To *Mugnaini* wood-fired pizza ovens."

"Of course, because only the best will do for my witch."

We touched glasses, drank, then tucked into the food in a companionable silence. Finally Xavier leaned back and sighed, patting his stomach.

"That was amazing. I wish you didn't have this catering job. We could cook, eat, and have sex all day, or week, or month, or forever."

The idea sounded oddly appealing, but as fast as I was falling for this demon, I knew that relationships could burn out in the blink of an eye, leaving me alone with the one thing that had never failed to give me solace in times of sorrow.

"I love my job." I told him. "You can't be the only one to enjoy my talents in the kitchen."

His eyebrows shot up. "And your talents in the bedroom?"

"Those I'll gift to you alone."

"You better." He got up and came around the table, pulling me off my stool and into his arms. "I don't like to share. If I can't be the sole recipient of your culinary skills, I better be the only one in your bed."

"So sex with other people in my van is okay?" I teased.

"Or a room in Hollister's Inn? Or that pond off Dillon's Bend Road?"

He smiled down at me, but something dark flickered in his blue eyes. "I'm changing my mind. You're too tempting to be around these mortals. I'm going to spirit you off to hell and lock you away where you'll always be mine."

I shivered a bit, searching his face. The darkness was gone, leaving the sexy demon I'd come to know the last few days. He could never take me by force. I might not have anything in the way of defensive or offensive magic, but my sisters did. They'd never let anyone hurt me. And if Xavier did drag me off to hell, I'm sure Cassie could get Lucien to do something about it. He *was* the son of Satan, after all.

But what if I went voluntarily? I had my career and my family, but what else was holding me here? Hell had always been portrayed in a terrifying light, but maybe there were nice areas that would be good for a holiday with a sexy demon. It could be like vacationing in Hawaii and checking out the volcanos. Would I have to be dead first? Could I squeeze a trip to hell in between catering jobs?

"I'm so busy." I reached up to put my hand on his cheek. "Maybe I can put a long weekend on the schedule sometime in the next few months."

He turned his head to kiss my palm. "And what if I want more than a long weekend?"

If the last few days were any indication, I would want more than a long weekend as well. I'd want a lifetime. How would that work? His job as a crossroads demon, and my booked-solid schedule? The goblin party hadn't been all that difficult to prep for, and the barbeque was mostly meat, but what would happen when I was spending every waking moment for weeks prepping food, attending events, and rushing home to clean before launching into more prep?

"Let's take it one day at a time." I moved his hands from my waist and took a step back.

One day at a time. And if some miracle occurred and this thing between us had staying power, well then maybe I'd do what I'd never considered before and start saying "no" to jobs. Maybe I'd make room in my life for more than just my career.

CHAPTER 13

GLENDA

I arrived just before noon, waving to Antwan as I hopped out of the van. He looked completely out of place—a tall, muscle-bound, bald, black man who looked like he should have been a CrossFit trainer or a bouncer standing in front of a putt-putt course. He'd moved to Accident five years ago but was more comfortable in the human world than most of our residents. He'd bought this putt-putt course, and construction was underway to build an old-fashioned arcade to the side, and he seemed to be happy in our community even though he took vacations a three or four times a year to head to the coast. No doubt our lakes and marshes weren't quite what the shark shifter was used to.

Antwan waved back, giving the parking lot a quick scan before opening the door for me.

"Everything good?" I asked him.

He nodded. "Your sister was here putting up the charms an hour ago. I made sure all my regulars knew today was a private party."

Bronwyn and Sylvie had partnered to work on a set of charms that would deter humans from even entering the parking lot. If any somehow managed to pass those, then Antwan would make sure they left before they saw anything.

And trust me, if Antwan asked someone to leave, they left. I'd grown up around trolls, werewolves, and even a dragon, but Antwan was the most intimidating person I'd ever met.

"Piffle is already here decorating," he added. "I'm gonna be minding the door most of the time, so make sure you save a plate for me."

My eyes widened. "Of gnome food? Slugs, turnips, bread, and sour cherry pie?"

His face settled into a thoughtful expression. "Never had slugs before. I like eel, though and I'm assuming it's similar? I'd be willing to give it a try."

Okay. Mental note: shark shifters like eel, and aren't adverse to trying unusual foods. "I'll put a few aside for you to try," I told him as I pulled my cart through the doorway.

Piffle was putting red pointed birthday hats on tables, her blonde braids nearly brushing the ground as she walked. The tables were set near a seven-foot pile of fake granite rocks, the dinosaur waterfall spewing neon blue water in the background.

Gnomes were famous for their gardening abilities. Flowers. Vegetables. They were especially good at growing root vegetables. I could get all sorts of heirloom varieties of veggies with flavor profiles absent in a world of supermarket foods. When I'd been told the birthday party was going to be here, I'd been surprised. Artificial turf, concrete rocks and animals, and plastic flora surrounded us. I guess the appeal was the game itself. Gnomes loved to play, and they had been able to talk about nothing but this party for over a month now. None of them had ever played putt-putt before, making this party just as much about the new game as it was Gronk's birthday celebration.

"Here?" I asked Piffle as I pulled a set of chafing dishes from the cart.

"The buffet goes on this table," she replied, braids bouncing as she trotted over to a long, low table.

I bent to put the chafing dishes down. The tallest gnomes were barely above my knee, although the tall pointed hats many of them liked to wear put them closer to my hip. Just as the food was tailored to their tastes, these tables were set for their height. Which meant I was probably going to need a chiropractor when I was done with this party. Or a massage.

My imagination was suddenly filled with visions of Xavier and naked massage. Both of us naked. And that massage leading to a couple of very happy endings. I shook off the thoughts and got down to work. I had a party to cater, and there was no way I was going to let naughty fantasies about a sexy demon interfere with my work.

The gnomes began arriving just as I'd set out the *schallea*. They socialized, then sang an off-key version of the birthday song, before drinking a glass of *schallea* in Gronk's honor. The birthday boy gave a short speech thanking everyone for attending, then instructed them all to get a golf club, a ball, and start playing.

Gnomes playing putt-putt had to be one of the most amusing things I'd seen this year. They took the game very seriously, behaving as if they were on the PGA tourney as they set up at each hole. A bogey resulted in cries of frustration and shaking the golf club at the sky. A hole in one seemed to require universal celebration, including a few moments of dancing. I'd never seen so many gnomes bounding around and "flossing" before today. Thankfully gnomes weren't competitive, and they celebrated every time one of them shouted "one!" and moaned when someone had a poor shot.

As they finished up, they all came through the buffet line,

eating bread and turnips as their first course. A few indulged in a second glass of *schallea*, and I sincerely hoped those gnomes were *not* driving back to Accident after the party.

Everyone made "ooo" noises as I put out the slugs. This had been the most complicated food of this party. They'd been sliced and marinated for twenty-four hours, then baked in the oven. I'd wrapped each slice of slug in pie crust, baking it again to make little slug pies. Just before serving, I poured the warm sauce over each pie. Even *I* thought they looked and smelled delicious, if only I didn't know what was inside the pastry shells.

The gnomes swarmed the buffet table and soon there was nothing but empty trays and happy gnomes, all patting their protruding bellies and stroking their beards. I began to prep the sour cherry pies while Scooter and Depper stood up to give speeches about Gronk's illustrious life, including some ribbing about a few of the old gnome's gardening faux pas over the centuries. As I put the pies on the table, I saw Scooter clutch his stomach and run off the stage. A few seconds later, Depper followed him. A trickle of fear raced down my back and I hoped that both gnomes suddenly had to pee.

They didn't. I'd barely begun to cut the pies and gnomes were running from the tables as if someone had screamed fire, but instead of screaming all I heard was retching.

Piffle staggered back in. Her face had a greenish cast and she gagged a little as she caught sight of the pies. I moved to block her view and asked her what was going on, not sure if I needed to break out some of my healing magic, or place an emergency call to Cassie or what.

"Slugs," she gasped, clasping a hand over her mouth. "Something…in…slugs."

"What can I do?" I asked Piffle. "I've got some healing

potions in the van that I can bring in. Or Tums? Seltzer water?"

The gnome retched a little at the mention of my potions. Although my smoothies were in high demand for serious injury, many decided they'd rather endure the discomfort of aches, pains, and head colds rather than deal with the foul taste. I wasn't sure if my magic would make any of the gnomes feel less queasy, but it certainly would help keep the vomiting at bay.

The vomiting. Poor Antwan. He'd need to clean upchuck off the artificial turf, the concrete sculptures, and especially the waterfall by the eighteenth hole.

"No. We'll be fine in an hour or so, once we get it all out of our system," Piffle told me with a wave of her hand. "It'll… It'll be okay."

No, it wouldn't. This had never happened to me before. I'd prepared all sorts of unusual foods for the supernatural beings of Accident, and never made any of them sick. I'd never even missed the mark—not once. My food was always delicious. Perfect. What had happened to make these slugs so horrible? I'd taken such care with the recipe, with the ingredients, with the preparation. This shouldn't have happened.

But it did, and clearly it was my fault.

I'd ruined Gronk's birthday party. Now probably wasn't the time to offer reparations, plus I needed time to think of what might be a suitable "I'm so sorry" for what seemed to have been massive food poisoning in the gnome community, but there was one thing I *could* do.

"I'm so terribly sorry." The words sounded less than adequate. "I'll figure out what happened and ensure this sort of thing never occurs again. Of course, I don't expect payment at all for the catering, and I'll be refunding your deposit. I'll get in touch with you in a few days and we can talk about what I can do to make this up to you."

Piffle clapped a hand over her mouth, nodding before she dashed off again. Knowing there was nothing I could do, I packed up, taking the sour cherry pies with me. I was pretty sure none of the gnomes would risk eating them after what had happened, and I couldn't stand for them to go to waste.

As I wheeled my cart toward the door, I saw Anwan standing in the parking lot, staring into the distance as if his glare alone could hold back any human that might dared to even venture down this road.

"You save any of those slugs for me?" he asked.

Tears blurred my vision. "Oh, Antwan, you don't want to eat those. Something's wrong with them. All the gnomes are sick. They're getting sick all over your putt-putt course."

Antwan didn't seem particularly bothered about the clean-up facing him after the gnomes left. Instead, he pursed his lips and with another narrow-eyed glance toward the road, took the foil-wrapped plate from my cart.

"This them?"

I nodded, too choked up to say anything.

He peeled the foil back and gave them a sniff, picking one up with two fingers.

"Don't do it, Antwan," I told him.

He shrugged. "I'm a shark. I can eat just about anything and be okay. Might not like it but won't make me sick. Not much makes me sick."

Before I could say another word, he popped the pastry-wrapped slug into his mouth and chewed thoughtfully. Nodding, another slug pastry followed the first.

"These are good," he said, picking up the third and last piece. "I'll definitely ask you to make some of these for me in the future. The coriander in the sauce really gives it an extra little kick."

Coriander?

I stared at him, horrified. Coriander was what the seeds

were generally called, where the leafy part of the plant was better known as cilantro or Chinese parsley. I hadn't used coriander seeds or any types of parsley in my cooking. I knew better. Gnomes could tolerate the leaves, although they always claimed cilantro tasted like soap to them, but the coriander seeds made them very ill. I knew that. There was no way I would have made such a mistake.

But my cooking was the only food served at this party. I couldn't deny the gnomes' gastro-intestinal issues were caused by anything else, especially given the reaction by every single attendee. Something had gone terribly wrong, and as mortified as I was, I couldn't deny responsibility. Whether it was my fault or not, I'd made and served this food, and the buck stopped with me.

Wait. I wasn't the only one who'd made this food. Suddenly I remembered Xavier at the engagement party, with his hand over the ginger cake, ready to infect it with something that would completely ruin the event. He'd helped with the slugs. He'd been the one who'd ground the spices and put together the sauce.

Three of my sisters had found love with demons, and one with a reaper, but that didn't mean all of hell's minions were equally kind, loyal, and loving. Humans, shifters, merfolk, heck even gnomes, came with all sorts of personalities— some of them good, and some of them not so good. I couldn't judge every demon I met by Lucien, Hadur, and Eshu standards.

I needed to face it, as wonderful as the last two days had been, Xavier was still a demon—a crossroads demon who made deals, took souls, and did all he could to wiggle his way around his contracts and make humans' lives miserable. There was no changing demon nature. I'd foolishly allowed a crossroads demon to help me with the most important thing in my life—my career. And I'd been stupid and prideful enough to enter into a second contest with him—one that would probably cost me my soul.

But I'd worry about my soul later. Right now I was facing a career-ending crisis.

I drove home and for the first time in my adult life, I didn't feel that sense of happiness and comfort as I entered my house. With a heavy heart, I unpacked the van and washed all the dishes. Then I made a pot of coffee, sat down with a mug and a slice of sour cherry pie, and cried. For a few hours I wallowed in my grief and despair. My reputation would be shot. No one would ever trust me to cater their events again. No one would ever eat anything I'd prepared again. My business would fold and I'd become a bitter, lonely witch cooped up in my house for the rest of my life. I had no real friends. I had no boyfriend. No one would care except my sisters who might show up once or twice a week to deliver groceries for a pity visit, being careful not to even drink a cup of coffee that my hands had touched. Then when I died, Xavier would come collect my soul and I'd spend an eternity being tormented in hell—which would probably be preferable to the lonely life I was envisioning.

After two pieces of pie and half a pot of coffee, I wasn't feeling particularly cheerful, but at least I'd stopped my drama-filled imagining of my future and started to feel something else. Anger, for one. If Xavier had truly messed with my slugs—and I couldn't imagine what else could have happened—then I was going to run him through my meat grinder feet-first. Then I was going to kick his ass at the werewolf barbeque and keep my soul. And somehow over the next few weeks, I was going to make things right with the gnomes. Never again would I let anyone in my kitchen, especially a demon. Never again.

In fact, I was never letting one in my house again. Not in my bed, not in my kitchen, not even on my front porch.

There was a knock at the door and I realized as I opened it that I was going to have to postpone my vow a bit because I really didn't want to have a screaming argument with Xavier in the middle of the street.

"So what are we cooking tonight?" Xavier wiggled his eyebrows at me as he walked in. "More wood-fired pizza?"

I was never having wood-fired pizza again. Either the real stuff or our euphemism.

"You've got some nerve showing up after what you did," I snapped. "How could you? How could you do that?"

He stopped, tilting his head and frowning. "It's what I do. I'm a crossroads demon. I thought you knew that. I make deals with people. I bargain for their souls and once the deal is sealed, I make their life miserable until I can collect upon their death."

I blinked back furious tears. "You asshole. You utter asshole. Stupid me, I thought things would be different, that somehow what we had would…I don't know, change you or something."

He froze, confusion on his face. "I am who I am, Glenda. I can't stop being a crossroads demon any more than you can stop using your magic and cooking up delicious food."

Delicious food. I instantly thought back to the gnomes racing from the party, every one of them made sick because of this guy.

"Get out," I snapped, shoving him toward the door. "Get out and don't come back."

His face revealed a moment of vulnerable pain before he closed it away and glared at me. "We still have a bet, witch. A deal is a deal, and I won't allow you to back out on me."

"Oh, I wouldn't dream of backing out. It's not like you've got a chance in hell of beating me anyway. I could out-cook you with my wand-hand tied behind my back."

He rolled his eyes. "Hardly. I *let* you win last time. I won't let you win this time." He took a step closer, crowding me. I caught my breath, struggling to keep from taking a step backward. I wouldn't give him the satisfaction of intimidating me, of making me move.

"I'll win. And then I'll have your soul."

Before I could wrestle my emotions enough to muster a reply he'd left, slamming my door so hard it rattled the house. I gritted my teeth, determined not to fall back into a flood of tears and spend the night drowning my sorrow in sour cherry pie. I needed to get my shit together. I needed to plan for the most amazing catering job of my life, to create food that would make the angels in heaven weep. I needed to make sure I won and kept my soul.

Which meant that I didn't need to be alone tonight with my very tumultuous thoughts. No, tonight of all nights, I needed my sisters.

CHAPTER 14

XAVIER

My anger faded before I was two blocks from Glenda's house, but I didn't have the courage to return and face her wrath and disappointment. How could she think that a few days in her company would completely change me? Did she truly expect me to give up everything I was to be with her? A part of me wondered if I even could. As demons, we reported to a higher power, and that higher power didn't exactly appreciate dereliction of duty. There had been a few exceptions over the ages. Occasionally a demon got trapped in an oil lamp, or a bottle, or a circle, and was basically on what amounted to an extended leave. Sometimes those individuals were forgotten for a while. Although everyone assumed they were still trapped, no one really checked up on them. I supposed that a demon could have been released on go the minion equivalent of AWOL, but I didn't know how that would work out in my case.

And why was I even thinking of this? I loved my work. I wasn't about to give it up for a sexy witch who made me feel all sorts of things I'd never felt before. A witch who wove her magic around me in the kitchen as well as in the bedroom.

Even now I longed to be with her, but not if she insisted I give up everything that made me a demon.

Damnation, I just didn't understand witches at all. But I knew one demon who did. All of hell had gossiped when he'd gone on vacation and bound a witch to his side. Although a lot of demons joked that it was the witch who'd bound Lucien to her side instead.

Being the son of Satan gave Lucien quite a lot of street cred, but snagging himself a witch had sent that reputation into the stratosphere. He was here in Accident. Everyone knew that, especially those who needed to contact him for business reasons. I could find him, but would he talk to me? Lucien was pretty high above my pay grade, but right now I needed someone who knew witches. I needed someone who could advise me how to get this crazy idea out of Glenda's head, to make her forgive me, make her love me, make her mine.

I zipped back to hell, bribed a few demons, then found myself back in Accident, standing in front of an old house that seemed to have a hodge-podge of additions stuck onto it. It didn't exactly look like the sort of place I'd expect the son of Satan to reside, but there was no accounting for tastes. Besides, I'd heard the guy was rather eccentric. Marching up the steps, I rang the doorbell and waited.

A woman answered. She had reddish brown hair, was wearing a business suit, and from the resemblance, I imme-diately realized she must be a relative of Glenda's. A cousin? A sister? We'd spent so much time cooking and flirting that I'd never asked her about her family. Of course this woman had to be some sort of relative though. Glenda was a witch. Lucien's bonded female was a witch. I doubted there were two witches in this town that *weren't* related.

"I'm here to see Lucien." I wasn't sure how I was supposed to address the demon's witch consort. As a crossroads demon, I'd been a bit out of the loop on affairs in hell, and I didn't know how formal their relationship was.

The witch spun around and motioned for me to follow. "He's in the kitchen. Are you from the second circle? I hope that acid situation is resolved because we've got plans this weekend. There is no way I'm going to let Lucien go running off to hell when we've got the werewolf barbeque and family dinner night. If you all can't get it straightened out by Friday, then it's just going to have to wait until Monday."

I stared at her back, a little shocked at her bossy tone. Not that I expected the son of Lucifer and Lilith would bond with a passive female, but this seemed excessive. I barely knew Lucien, but he must be a very strong demon to control this woman.

Or perhaps those demons in hell were right, and the witch was wearing the pants in this relationship.

"Lucien!" the woman shouted as she entered the kitchen. "Some flunky from hell to see you, even though it's after five o'clock."

I half expected him to turn around and fry her to ash on the spot for such insubordination, but instead Lucien dried his hands on a kitchen towel and commented drily, "It's not like you don't bring work home with you, Cassie. I'll be at the barbeque, and I'll be here for family dinner, but some- times I need to work on the weekends."

The demon turned, clearly not recognizing me from his perplexed frown. Not that I'd expected him to know who I was. I bowed, then with a quick glance at the witch, spoke in Enochian, hoping that she wouldn't understand me.

"Son of Satan, I am in service as a crossroads demon, and I beg for your assistance in a matter of importance."

He shot a quick glance at the witch he'd called Cassie and nodded, replying in English. "I totally forgot about our meeting."

The witch narrowed her eyes. "Lucien, it's date night. We've got plans."

Lucien held up his hands. "I know, I know. Just give me an hour to meet with Freddy here. I'll make it up to you I promise."

Freddy?

"Yes, it will only take an hour." I turned my sexiest smile at the witch and saw a familiar spark in her eyes. Then I turned and saw a very clear warning in *Lucien's* eyes. Noted. No flirting with the witch belonging to the son of Lucifer.

He grabbed my arm and steered me out the front door and to a dark gray SUV in the driveway. I climbed in the passenger side and we rode in silence outside the wards to a little diner next to an entrance ramp onto the highway.

"We've got to make this quick," Lucien told me. "The town is full of shifters, and they can hear a pin drop from six blocks away. I'm assuming whatever you've got to tell me isn't something we want known outside of hell, so this is the safest place to talk. We've only got an hour though." He checked his watch. "Actually, we've only got about ten minutes. I've got to be back for date night or Cassie will skin me alive."

I choked back a laugh, wondering exactly how powerful this witch of his was. But since we only had ten minutes, I didn't have time to ask questions—well, questions beyond the ones I'd originally planned to ask.

"I need to know about witches. Did your witch ask you to give up your work in hell? Or change who you are? Is that a reasonable request?"

Lucien's eyes widened. "I thought...you're not from the second circle? Or the fourth? This isn't about the acid or the three souls that managed to escape?"

"No. I'm a crossroads demon, and I met a witch last Saturday. I'm...fond of her. And I thought she was fond of me, but she just threw me out and told me never to come back because she'd expected me to change." I ran a hand through my hair. "Did your witch do this?"

A look of amusement flitted across Lucien's face and he leaned back in the booth, signaling for the waitress to come over. "What's your name?"

"I go by Xavier right now."

He nodded, asking the waitress for two coffees and two slices of cherry pie before turning back to me. "What did you do to piss her off, Xavier?"

I shook my head. "Just my job. We had an amazing night together. I left in the morning and had to go do all the things that had been pushed back while I spent time with her."

Lucien chuckled. "That's normal. I can't tell you how I scramble to fit in everything while Cassie is at work. It's not easy, but she expects me to be there for her when she's home and not be running off on hell's business all the time. It's the price you pay for being with a witch."

"I had two contracts I needed to make, six souls to collect and deliver to the appropriate circle of hell for eternal punishment, then I had to contact eight prospective candidates concerning a possible future contract." I let out a frustrated breath. "It was a busy day. And all I wanted to do when I got to her house was enjoy some private time, if you know what I mean."

"Oh I know." Lucien waited as the waitress gave us our pie and coffee.

I poured some disgusting non-dairy creamer into mine and took a sip, hiding a grimace. Then I ate a bite of pie. It was…okay. Too sweet, and the cherries were obviously canned with that nasty gel that constitutes a filler. The crust was made with shortening, which can be delightfully flaky if done correctly. This wasn't bad, but it wasn't what I'd call good either. And it certainly wasn't up to the level I'd come to expect in the last few days.

"Glenda's is better," I muttered. "I really wanted some of that sour cherry pie she made for the gnomes. I was hoping to have a few pieces tonight."

"Glenda?" Lucien nearly choked on his pie laughing. "That's who you're mooning over? Glenda?"

I felt myself bristle. "She beautiful, and her magic is in everything she touches. From the first moment when she slapped my hand and told me I couldn't befoul her ginger cake, I knew I wanted her to be mine."

"Why would you want to mess with Glenda's ginger cake? That's got to be one of the best desserts I've ever tasted." Lucien took a bite of his pie and looked down at the pastry mournfully. I realized I wasn't the only one noting the difference between this and Glenda's creations.

"I was going to poison the food to torment a man whose soul I've been waiting to collect, but the moment I tasted it I forgot all about my victim and found myself trapped by her magic, her beauty, those amazing prime-rib sandwiches. You should have tasted the chicken pesto sandwich she made me yesterday."

Lucien nodded. "Glenda's cooking *is* amazing. Honestly, I don't know that much about her other than she's one of Cassie's younger sisters and her magic involves healing. She's not around the house as much as the other sisters. Other than a few occasions here and there, I only see her during Sunday family dinner."

"You're bound to a witch," I insisted. "I was hoping you could give me advice. Pointers. Did your witch demand that you give up your job? Being a demon? That you deny your father and walk away from your infernal inheritance?"

"No, although as I said, she does get irritated when my position in hell interferes with date night. Or Sunday family dinner. Other than that, she's been as supportive of my work as I am of her position in Accident as head witch."

I sighed. "I enjoy the time I spend with Glenda. Being with her feels right. But I can't imagine not being a cross-roads demon."

"What exactly does she object to about your job?"

I held my hands up. "I've got no idea. Everything was fine when I left. She knew I had work to do, but I didn't specify what and she didn't ask. Then when I came by later, she threw me out."

Lucien shrugged. "Could be she'd just had a bad day? Try again tomorrow, and maybe she'll have forgotten all about… whatever it was she thinks you did."

"Really? That's what I should do?"

"Sure. It's better than moping around or asking me for advice." Lucien gave up and pushed the half-eaten pie aside. "How about I talk to Cassie? I can have her speak to Glenda and see if she can smooth things over? I can't promise anything will come of it, but it may help."

I thought for a moment. "I don't think that would do any good, but I'd be grateful for any help. There's something else you need to know, though. We have a contract, a contest. Whoever wins gets what they most desire."

Lucien choked on his coffee. "You can't take her soul. Cassie would kill me if I let a demon take one of her sister's souls."

I frowned, wondering if he was speaking figuratively.

"I wouldn't be so foolish," I reassured the other demon. "As much as I want her soul, I know that I'd never be allowed to keep it. The thought of her soul in the possession of another demon, of him doing whatever he wished with her… that is something I could never allow to happen."

Lucien leaned back in the booth. "Then what exactly did you intend on demanding if you won?"

I squirmed, unable to admit to Lucien what I really wanted. It would make me sound weak, like a fool. He was right. I was mooning over a witch, wanting things that I'd never have. I should bail on the contest, but the part of me that was a crossroads demon would never allow that to happen. Instead I'd need to think of something else for my prize, because of course I'd win. I had the power of hell behind me. I'd win and I'd ask for something like a ginger cake, or a catered dinner for two, and then maybe Glenda would give me another chance.

"I haven't decided yet," I confessed, a mixture of emotions roaring through me. Excitement that I'd be seeing Glenda again in three days whether she wanted to see me or not. Eager anticipation to try whatever she was making for our challenge. And fear.

Fear about what she'd do when I won.

Fear about what I'd do when I had to accept I'd lost everything I wanted.

GLENDA

"Men suck. Demons suck." I downed the tequila shot and slammed it on the bar.

"Hell, yeah!" Adrienne followed my example, not even flinching as she threw the shot down her throat. My sister had answered my plea for help, showing up at Pistol Pete's dressed in her tan Perkins Wildlife Control shirt and followed by one of the biggest vultures I'd ever seen.

I hadn't asked. And now I really wasn't in any condition to ask. Clearly my tolerance for alcohol had gone way down over the years, while Adrienne's had held up. She was drinking me under the table. And that buzzard was eyeing me with a judging expression I really didn't appreciate.

"What?" I snapped at the bird. "I'm not drunk. I'm just…relaxed."

I swear the vulture raised an eyebrow. Did vultures have eyebrows? Maybe I should Google that. I got out my phone, but my fingers didn't seem to be working right and I ended up with a whole lot of links for Vulcan stoves and articles about Leonard Nimoy.

Hmmm. Vulcan stoves.

"So what exactly did this demon do?" Adrienne ran a finger around the rim of her shot glass.

"Nearly destroyed my career. I'm going to become a celibate. No dating. No sex. Just cooking and work. Maybe I'll take up stained glass or something if I need a hobby. Or go back to rock climbing."

Adrienne jerked her head toward me. "Your career? He messed with your appliances? Your cooking?"

The expression of horror on her face was vindicating. She understood.

I'd always considered myself equally close to all of my sisters, but in my moment of need, I'd decided to call on the ones who wouldn't be in a position where they felt they had to defend their demon mates. Ophelia's dude Nash wasn't technically a demon, but she was working tonight. Sylvie's Eshu was some weird not-a-demon-but-a-demon, but he also had loose lips and was well known for causing a roller-coaster of chaos. Plus Sylvie was a therapist and I really didn't need her analysis of my childhood, commitment issues, and sex life right now.

That left Adrienne and Babylon. Adrienne had arrived at the bar first, with the vulture in tow. Babylon said she was on her way.

"He sabotaged the gnome birthday party catering job," I told my sister. "Coriander in the slugs. They all ended up vomiting. Ruined the whole event and probably ruined my reputation. I'm going to do my best to make it up to them, but it will probably take years before any of the supernaturals in Accident trust me with any specialized dietary needs."

Adrienne sucked in a breath and gestured for the bartender. "Sheesh, Glenda. That's horrible. Why would he do that?"

I shrugged, tears blurring my vision. "Because that's who he is. He's a crossroads demon and he torments humans who have made deals with him. We had a wonderful two days cooking and talking and laughing and…you know."

"Sex?" Adrienne saluted me with the empty shot glass, a sly grin on her face.

"Yes, sex." I felt my face heat up at the thought. I'd slept with him. We'd done a whole lot more than sleeping. I'd actually had sex with someone on top of one of my stainless steel prep tables—that's how much this demon had enthralled me.

The vulture made a grunting noise and Adrienne rolled her eyes. "Oh shut it, Drake."

"Drake?" I frowned down at the judgey vulture.

"I named him after the singer," Adrienne confessed. "Isn't he cute? He's been following me around for the last few weeks. Last night I woke up to find him perched on the headboard of my bed."

That was super creepy. I gave the vulture another glare then turned to the bartender, ordering a second round of shots. Or maybe it was the third?

"Anyway, I was stupid enough to trust him. It was just like all the other guys—they fall in love with my food—and you know I can't resist a man that loves my food."

"He's hot?" Adrienne prodded. "Everyone is in love with your food. It can't just be that."

It wasn't. "Yes, he's hot. And he showed up at my house two days after I met him, trying to get me to make a deal with him, to wager my soul. I refused, and he ended up staying all day and helping me cook. We had…we had so much fun." My voice hitched thinking of how I'd felt working with Xavier by my side. We'd talked. We'd laughed. And the sexual tension had grown with every passing hour. I'd been such a fool.

"He came back the next day and helped again," I continued. "That's when we ended up in bed. All night. He was gone this morning, and I got everything loaded and ready for the gnome party. We were the only two who touched those slugs. It had to have been him who added the coriander. I caught him trying to tamper with my ginger cake the first time we met, so I know that's his thing. I'm such an idiot to have trusted him, to have slept with him."

Adrienne patted my shoulder. "Glenda, don't be so hard on yourself. I've slept with all sorts of losers. It happens. I'll help make things right with the gnomes. I took care of a mole problem for them last year and they owe me one." The vulture grunted again and my sister reached around to toss the bird a peanut. "You were right to kick him out, though. Good riddance. If he shows up again, I'll give him a case of lice he'll never forget."

I grimaced. "Actually he's going to be at the werewolf barbeque."

Adrienne's eyes narrowed. "Then I'll make sure the lice are ready."

That made me giggle. Then I remembered the stupid wager I'd made, and that wiped the smile right off my face. "I'd appreciate that, but I'm not sure how much good it will do. I betted him that I could make a better brisket. Winner gets whatever they want."

Adrienne nearly choked on her peanuts. "You made a deal with him? A crossroads demon? Oh, Glenda, how could you?"

"Like I said. I was an idiot. I trusted him. We made a bet that day about who could make the best lunch, and I won. It was flirty and sexy and I just assumed this bet would be the same." I bit my lip, really wanting another shot of tequila. "But I think if he wins this bet, he'll want my soul."

The vulture hissed and power whipped around Adrienne, her aura shifting to blue and violet. "Over my dead body. None of us will let that happen, Glenda. Cassie won't let that happen. She's banging the son of Satan. That's got to pull some weight."

"But I made a deal. I voluntarily agreed to this. Hell, I was the one that proposed it." I stared glumly down at my empty shot glass. "I don't think Lucien, or any of you can help me. I just need to make the best brisket ever, and hope Xavier's isn't better."

"You'll win," Adrienne announced. "If it has to do with food, you'll win."

There was an edge of worry in her voice that told me she wasn't as confident as she seemed. I had two days until the werewolf barbeque—two days to work my magic and try to save my soul. And after I won, I'd let Adrienne lice that demon and banish him from Accident forever.

The front door flung open and I along with Adrienne and the other three occupants of the bar turned to see a petite red-haired witch burst into the bar. She had on a black mini skirt and a black tank-top with a white skull imprinted across the front.

Babylon. The youngest of my sisters, and the only Perkins in known memory to be gifted with the skill of necromancy. She stopped halfway through the bar, staring at the vulture.

"Whoa! That is one sick bird, Addy. Where'd you get him?"

As witches we were all a little on the odd side, but Babylon with her affinity for the dead was the sister even *we* considered weird. Adrienne was like Snow White on steroids with her animal communication skills. Ever since she'd been a child she'd been collecting animal friends, and not just the fuzzy and feathered woodland creature kind either. Addy liked bugs and creepy crawlies just as much as she did the cute animals. The only thing stranger than seeing your sister best friends with a swarm of wasps or a nest of spiders was seeing your youngest sister animating corpses.

"That's Drake." Adrienne made the introductions and Babylon knelt down to put herself at eye level with the bird. It wasn't something I'd do, given how sharp Drake's beak looked.

"I love vultures!" Babylon exclaimed. "This is way cooler than the time you had that colony of fire ants in your backyard."

"I miss the fire ants," Addy said with noticeable regret. "Stupid neighbor and his lawn chemicals."

"These guys can pick a carcass squeaky clean in an hour," Babylon informed me. "Their beaks are like freakin scapels."

"Nice to know." I eyed the bird's beak with renewed respect.

"Can you bring him over next week sometime?" Babylon asked Adrienne. "I want to do a skeleton army of mice, and it would be so much easier with his help. Better than trying to boil all their flesh off, especially since a few of them are a bit ripe."

Annnnd it was time to change the subject before I barfed up my tequila.

"How about you guys keep the disgusting details of that project for later, okay?" I patted one of the stools. "Belly up to the bar, Lonnie. We're drinking tequila. Or have we switched back to beer?"

"Tequila is totally my jam. What did I miss?" my youngest sister asked, squeezing between Adrienne and me. "How many drinks have you had yet? Damn it, I'm behind. Pete! I need to catch up. Send two shots of tequila my way and get us all another round."

We caught her up on the news as Babylon slammed down two shots of tequila. By the time Adrienne had told her about my latest bet with Xavier, we were all facing a third shot of tequila.

"No biggie. You're absolutely going to win this thing with

sexy-crossroads-demon," Babylon told me. "No one's food comes close to yours. The gnome thing will blow over in a few days, and you'll wipe the floor with this demon at the werewolf party."

"Let's drink to that!" Adrienne lifted her shot glass and Lonnie and I did the same.

The tequila didn't burn like the first two shots had. Instead a pleasant warmth spread through me and I smiled, suddenly feeling like everything was right in the world. Although a tiny bit of my brain was well aware that come tomorrow morning, I'd probably have the worst hangover ever.

"So, what do you want?" Babylon asked me. "When you win, what are you going to ask him to do for you? Or give you?" She winked. "Or do *to* you?"

I blinked, suddenly envisioning a re-do of the last few days. Not the sort of re-do where I slammed the door in Xavier's face and never even let him in. No, the sort of re-do where he didn't tamper with the slugs, and the gnome party had been a huge it. I'd come home, and when he'd arrived, we'd eat the leftover sour cherry pie, then made love. And when I woke up, he was there.

That's what I wanted. But it wasn't going to happen, and I didn't want to admit to my sisters that I had somehow managed to fall for a demon I'd met four days ago, and feared I'd never get over him. Ever.

"I don't know if what you want is possible," Adrienne said, making me wonder if mind-reading was one of her talents. "He sounds like a total ass, Glenda. You can do better. Ask him for something ridiculously extravagant when you win, then boot his ass to the curb."

My mind immediately went to the Mugnaini wood-fired pizza oven.

Babylon shrugged. "Personally, I like asshole guys. I think

you should go for it. When you win, make him your love slave for a few weeks. Just make sure you stipulate that he needs to stay out of your kitchen."

"My kitchen is most of my house," I protested.

"No biggie. Just confine him to the bedroom," Babylon said. "That's where you want him anyway."

My mind immediately went to Xavier and me on top of my stainless steel table and I felt myself flush. But that wasn't just where I wanted him. It wasn't just sex. If it had been, I wouldn't be so upset. No, we'd had a camaraderie, a connection—at least I'd thought we had. That's why I felt so betrayed by his sabotage of the slugs.

Suddenly I didn't want to talk about Xavier any more. Or think about him. I didn't want to remember how alive I'd felt the last two days when we'd been together. I didn't want to go back to my house that suddenly seemed so empty and bleak.

I'd vented. I'd had my pity party and gotten support from my sisters. Now it was time to move on.

"You're both coming to the werewolf barbeque, right?" I asked. "I'm making some really amazing stuff—not just the brisket."

Babylon and Adrienne exchanged a glance.

"We'll be there," Adrienne said, and I knew that it wasn't just because of the food, or because this was a special event in our town. She'd be there for me. And so would Babylon.

So would all my sisters. Xavier might get my soul, but if he won, I was sure that six witches would make his eternal life a living nightmare.

"Thanks." I flagged Pete down again, deciding that we might want to switch to beer if any of us were to have a chance of making it out of the bar on our own two feet.

"Lice," Adrienne reminded me. "The guy is going to have

a whole lot of lice. And I might have Drake shit on his head as well."

"Zombies," Babylon added. "He'll have a hard time getting anything done with a pack of zombies following him around. Plus they stink. Oh, and they attract a lot of flies."

"Flies are good." Adrienne nodded. "Flies and lice. That demon will rue the day he ever screwed with a Perkins witch. Or screwed a Perkins witch."

I laughed, then ordered a round of beers. Sisters. My love life might be in shambles, my heart bruised, my career reputation smudged, but no matter what, my sisters would always be there for me.

Always.

CHAPTER 16

GLENDA

I slept in Thursday, indulging in my hangover until well past noon. Then I drug my sorry butt out of bed, got a shower, forced down what food my rebellious stomach could tolerate, and headed up Heartbreak Mountain. Veering off a back road, I circled around the west side of the mountain to Clinton's compound. There hadn't been any improvements over the last month mostly because part of the peace treaty between the wolf packs meant Clinton's group would be moving to their fifty acres on Savior Mountain next month, and every effort had gone into building a new compound on what was nothing more than rocks, trees, and briars. So far a new alpha house had been roughed out, and land cleared for a dozen temporary housing structures, but that was it. There wasn't much time for them to get everything reasonably livable, but now that Dallas' compound had been rebuilt, I was hoping some of his pack would pitch in and help Clinton. After all, it was in their best interests to get the other, smaller pack off Heartbreak Mountain and established in their own territory.

Word of my arrival must have preceded me, because

Clinton was out front of the alpha house, waiting for me. I parked and pulled one of the sour cherry pies from the back seat of my van.

Clinton sniffed the air appreciatively as we greeted each other. "I hope that's for me, because it smells darned good."

"It is." I handed him the pie. There was another in the backseat for Dallas. No sense in having six pies go to waste at my house, and I certainly couldn't eat them all myself.

"I just wanted to talk to you about the barbeque this weekend," I began as we made our way into the alpha house. "First, what sort of desserts are your favorite? I want to put a special something together for each alpha to honor the peace between the packs."

Clinton looked a bit flustered. "Well…since you're asking, I really like cakes. Growing up, my Ma would bake cakes for pack functions, and she always made a little one just for me. I was too young to attend back then, and having that cake made me feel included. It made me feel like I was part of the pack, one of the grown-ups. Plus, having my own personal cake…it made me special. Loved."

I smiled, thinking how many of our favorite foods were tied up in childhood memories, like my pinwheels.

"Is any particular cake your favorite?" I asked.

He shook his head. "Ma made all kinds. She had a big book of recipes that had been in her family for ages. I should ask Tink to get it to me. Hoping someday I can make a few of those for my pups, although I'm nowhere near the baker my Ma was."

My mind was already thinking of possibilities, but there were a couple of other things I needed to talk to Clinton about before I got going.

"I also wanted to let you know that there is going to be a contest. A…a demon and I are competing for who makes the best brisket, and you, your father, and Tink are the judges."

His eyes gleamed. "I love brisket. Looking forward to that one."

"Great!" Now for the difficult topic. "And last of all, Shelby and Stanley will be coming to the barbeque since it's a community-wide event and held on the land granted as public to all werewolves. I'd like to ask you and your father to make a special effort to welcome them, to be seen chatting with them a few times while they're in attendance. It would go a long way toward showing the other werewolves that you and Dallas really *are* including lone wolves in this new treaty. It's sort of a lead-by-example thing."

I was nowhere near as good at this sort of negotiation as Sylvie was, and that was made clear by the way Clinton's muscles all seemed to stiffen.

"Ain't gonna say anything nasty or throw them out but asking me to welcome them is a bit much."

"No, it's not." Here's where I put my foot down as a witch of Accident. "You're an alpha, Clinton. It's up to you to set an example and do things you don't want to do for the good of the pack."

A muscle in his jaw worked a bit and he glared at me. "Fine. I'll welcome them both. Maybe I'll even stop and say a few words to them, but I'm not being all buddy-buddy with either one. Shelby tried to kill me, and Stanley's a traitor."

"And if you and your pack want to remain in Accident, you need to put that behind you and act like an alpha."

Those were harsh words, and completely out of character for me. I had no idea why I was suddenly channeling Cassie. Maybe the fight with Xavier yesterday had me feeling more prickly than usual. Either way it worked. Clinton swallowed a few times and agreed to at least treat Stanley and Shelby as he would any other werewolf. I left feeling as if I'd actually accomplished something besides cooking and headed the other way up the mountain to my next stop.

Dallas wasn't at my meeting, but Tink was. I assumed since their mating ceremony that she spoke for him as the female alpha of the pack, and that this was how they'd decided to divide their duties. I quickly learned that Dallas was a pie werewolf who would truly love the sour cherry pie I'd brought, and that Tink was especially fond of those box-of-chocolates sweets from the human world—especially the ones with cream fillings.

I reversed the order of my topics a bit and broached the issue of Shelby and Stanley next. Tink waved it all away, promising me she'd take care of it and make sure Dallas was more than polite. Relieved that had gone well, I told her about the contest with the brisket.

She squealed and did a little dance. "That is fun! And I get to be the swing vote! Of course you'll win, but it's still a great idea. Brisket. Yum. So, who's this demon challenging Glenda the More-Than-Good? Guy is either an idiot or he's a pretty darned good cook himself. I'm hoping for the latter since I've got to actually eat this brisket of his."

"I've had his food. He's good." The words were said between clenched teeth. He was good. And for the first time in my life I was scared someone might be better than me. It wasn't just about my soul, it was the thought that a talent I held nearly sacred, one that set me apart from everyone else, might not be the best. Screw my magic, what I truly felt pride in was my cooking. It was what I lived for.

When had that happened? I'd always loved culinary arts, but I'd never used to pin my entire existence on it.

Tink gave me a hard look. "Thinking you've had more than his food. Tell me about this guy, Glenda, 'cause it seems like there's a story here."

I'd never been that close to Tink. Actually I hadn't even known exactly who she was until a few months ago, but somehow I found myself spilling my guts to her. I told her all about the engagement party where I'd first met Xavier. I told her about the two idyllic days we'd spent cooking and flirting and enjoying each other's company. I told her, without an indecent amount of detail, about the sex. And then I told her about the gnomes and Xavier's betrayal, and how I was now trapped into a contest with a demon I felt might just take my soul.

Tink nodded. "You want me to be impartial, or to vote for you? 'Cause if you need my vote, you got it."

"No. I need to win this fair. I'm the one that suggested this contest. If I can't win it on my own merits, then I didn't really win. He'll know that, and more than that, I'll know that."

The werewolf nodded. "Okay, but if you need me, Glenda, then you got me. You got the pack. Things are gonna be different now that I'm mated to Dallas. We're part of Accident. We might choose to live on our own, and keep to our traditions in some ways, but we're part of this community. We'll be there for you witches, just as we'll be there for any other group in Accident."

My eyebrows shot up. "Dallas is on board with this?"

Tink grinned. "Partially. Give me another month or two, and he'll be there."

Werewolves. Sheesh.

"Thanks Tink," I told her. "I'll see you on Saturday."

"I'll see you on Saturday," she replied, and somehow it sounded more like a vow of comradery than just a simple goodbye.

CHAPTER 17

GLENDA

On the way back I ran by Petunia's to check on Stanley, using the excuse that I needed to buy beer. Petunia's only sold beer, bait, and car parts as well as performing car repair. My van was in working order, and I didn't fish, so beer it was.

I parked and wove my way past the cars and trucks waiting to be repaired as well as those owned by the people buying bait and/or beer. Inside there were two goblins arguing about mealworms, a banshee looking through a book of car parts muttering something about brake pads for an '09 Malibu, and a gargoyle pulling a six-pack of Coors Light out of the cooler. A pixie flitted over top of Petunia's head as the boar shifter replaced the battery cables on an old pick-up truck. Two legs stuck out from under the front of a Mazda Miata, and for a second I had a flashback to last Saturday night.

Stanley wheeled out from under the Miata. "Hey, Petunia? We got a head gasket for this thing?"

"Trapper, go in the back and grab Stanley a J9691P5. Third row, fifth section, second shelf from the bottom,"

Petunia told the pixie.

Trapper disappeared in a flash of light and a rain of glitter. The boar shifter cursed, and ran a hand over his head, brushing the glitter to the ground.

"Leaving money for this beer on the counter, Petunia," the gargoyle called out, waving a fist full of bills.

I went over to the cooler and surveyed the beer options. Domestic. Craft. Guinness.

"Hey, Glenda!" Trapper buzzed by me with something that looked like a metal modern art sculpture encased in vacuum-sealed plastic.

Stanley snatched the part as the pixie dropped it mid-flight, then grinned over at me. "Getting some beer, Glenda?"

I nodded, randomly pulling a six pack out of the cooler. "Ring me up, Stanley? I've only got a twenty."

He set the car part down and came over to the cash register, scooping up the money the gargoyle had left behind and putting it in the drawer before ringing me up.

"Things okay, Stanley?" I asked in a soft voice as I handed him my twenty.

"Yeah." He grinned at me. "No more notes or threats or anything. Probably because of the wards around my house, and the deputies driving by, and Cassie occasionally standing outside like she's going to set the world on fire if anyone so much as lets their dog poop on my yard."

"Good." I took my change and stuffed it into my purse. "I spoke with Tink and Clinton, and they promised to support you and Shelby on Saturday."

Stanley gripped the counter tightly. "Might not stay too long, Glenda. Even if Dallas and Clinton are okay, I still know a lot of the others aren't gonna be friendly. And Bart... I made him promise not to come. I don't want to jeopardize his position in the pack."

I picked up my beer. "Thanks, Stanley. Even if you just

stay twenty minutes, it will help. I truly think Accident needs to become a place where lone wolves can be welcome, and as difficult as this is, you and Shelby are blazing the trail."

His smile was sad. "I never wanted to blaze trails, I just wanted to live my life. But if this is the path I'm on, then I'm gonna walk it like a wolf."

I left feeling deflated, even though just ten minutes ago I'd been flying high. Everything would eventually work out for the werewolves and Accident. I might not have Ophelia's divination talent, but I clearly saw where the future of our town was heading. Still, I hated that this change was causing so much pain. Everyone felt the aches of this transformation, but Stanley and Shelby, and even Alberta, were feeling it in spades.

My mood dived even further downward as I saw who was standing beside my van.

Xavier took a step to the side and held his hands up. "Before you chew me out, this is a public place. You don't have a restraining order out against me, and I have every right to be here."

"So are you here to buy beer, bait, or car parts?" I wasn't sure if I wanted to approach close enough to get into my car or stay where I was.

He eyed the beer in my hand. "Is that your secret ingredient in your brisket marinade?"

I couldn't help it. He'd seriously damaged my career and acted as if it wasn't a big deal. He'd excused his actions with "I'm a demon. It's what I do". I couldn't trust him. I shouldn't even speak to him. But my heart beat faster as I saw him by my car and warmth settled down low in my abdomen at the sound of his voice.

Beer. He'd said something about the beer. I glanced down at the six pack of Guinness. "I'm not telling you anything about my brisket recipe. Now move so I can get into my car."

"I'm not hindering you from getting into your car." He took another step to the side. "How about we work together on our brisket preparations? I'll even make you lunch. And dinner. And bring wine. I've got quite a nice wine cellar, I'll have you know."

I missed him. I missed this. I missed the banter, the companionship. But he'd betrayed me and I couldn't let that go. How many relationships had I turned a blind eye to the red flags? I needed to learn from the past and realize that Xavier was demon and he'd never change, no matter how charming I found him.

"Afraid you're going to lose?" I took a few steps forward and unlocked the car. "You want to work with me so you can steal my ideas? Xavier, even if I wrote down exactly what I was doing and you copied it exactly, you still wouldn't beat me. This is my talent. Food is everything to me."

"Everything?" He stepped forward and took the beer from my hand, putting it into the back seat of the van. "That's sad, Glenda. You're so much more than your cooking, no matter how amazing it is. I'm not trying to copy your recipes, I just want to spend time with you."

I yanked opened up the driver's door, which put me far too close to the demon. "Doesn't matter. I can't forgive what you did. The one thing that matters to me…. How could you do that after the time we'd spent together? How could you?"

He stepped into me, inches from my body, his breath fanning my face. "I'm the same demon you met at Benjamin Frederick Allen's party last week. I'm the same demon who helped you cook slugs and turnips, who made love to you six times. Glenda, you can't ask me to change who I am, just as I can't ask you to change who you are."

I clenched my jaw, blinking back tears and turning away so Xavier didn't see them. He had a point. He had a very valid point. "I'm not asking you to change, Xavier. I just…I just didn't think about who you were when I got into this…thing we had together. It was amazing, and I honestly wish things were different, but I can't see myself having anything long-term with someone who can do what you did and not even feel remorse about it. I can't. I'm sorry. I didn't mean to lead you on or anything, I just got caught up in the moment and didn't stop to think about how incompatible we are."

I climbed into the car, shutting the door before he could reach out to me.

"We're not incompatible, Glenda!" he shouted.

I choked back a sob, started my car, and backed out of the parking lot, refusing to look at Xavier, refusing to listen to what he was shouting.

We were incompatible. And I wasn't going to give a second chance to someone who'd hurt me so badly. I'd done that before and spent two weeks face-down in a gallon of Rocky Road ice cream when that relationship had gone down in flames.

I wouldn't suffer that sort of hurt again. Never again.

CHAPTER 18

GLENDA

Once home I surveyed my kitchen and wrote down everything I wanted to make for the barbeque, deciding what I could prep ahead of time, what needed to be done the night before, and what should be finished right before the barbeque started. Most of the dishes I was preparing would be done tomorrow, but there was a lot of prep work I could do now, including the dry rub for the brisket.

As I chopped vegetables, marinated chicken, and put some meat in the smoker for pulled pork, I kept thinking of Xavier.

He'd come to see me. He'd tracked me down and waited outside Petunia's to talk to me. Even though I'd accused him of wanting to spy on my brisket recipe, I knew that wasn't why he had wanted to come over. He missed me. I missed him. We would have such fun cooking together, trying to hide what we were doing as we put together our dry rub ingredients, as we chose what specific pieces of meat we would use for the contest versus the ones that would be served to the other attendees. We'd laugh. We'd flirt. We'd make love.

I wanted to forgive him, to give him another chance—give *us* another chance. I'd do just that, but there needed to be boundaries. It bothered me that he hadn't even apologized for what he'd done. He didn't seem to see that there was anything wrong with it at all. I couldn't be with someone who would hurt me and then shrug it off as being a demon. Bronwyn, Ophelia, and Sylvie wouldn't put up with that. Cassie most definitely wouldn't put up with that. She'd given her old boyfriend Marcus dozens of second chances, but as a panther shifter he could never be physically faithful to my sister no matter how much he loved her. Cassie finally ended the relationship. She couldn't be with someone who wasn't faithful, and Marcus couldn't change.

Even if Xavier promised, *would* he be able to change? I couldn't build a loving relationship unless he did change, and so far he'd shown no signs of even being willing to entertain the idea.

I'd need to accept him for who he was or walk away. And it was killing me to walk away.

Trying to keep my mind off Xavier, I got to work on the desserts.

Every werewolf would be enthusiastic about any meat dish I prepared, and I was also supplying enough vegetable and grain-based foods to cover the broad tastes of the other Accident residents who would be in attendance. But desserts...those were special. Each werewolf had their favorites, and in keeping with the theme of peace and togetherness, I was determined to provide a sweet that would satisfy each alpha.

Tink had said that Dallas loved pies. Since he was a bit of a traditionalist, I decided to make an apple pie in his honor. I had a dozen incredible recipes, though, and spent hours poring over them, trying to decide which one would wow the womanizing and fierce werewolf. Finally I decided to make two kinds. One would have a buttery, flaky crust and ribbons of caramel sweetening up tart apples. The other would use equally tart apples, but I'd make the crust with some extra sharp cheddar. And just because I was in an apple mood, I hauled three bushels of Golden Delicious apples from the cellar and made applesauce. These apples were a bit watery, but sweet enough that no added sugar was needed. Just a dash of grated cinnamon and a hint of vanilla extract, and the crock of applesauce went into the walk-in fridge.

The sun had set long ago, but I kept working, knowing that if I went to bed I'd only stare at the ceiling for hours thinking of Xavier. Checking on the pork loins in the smoker, I put the applesauce in the fridge, and moved the pies to a rack to cool.

Time to make a cake. Clinton was more modern in his tastes than his father, but he appreciated tradition and in some ways was just as nostalgic. I looked over my recipes, discarding the ones for chocolate fudge with a bittersweet ganache and my favorite old-fashioned carrot cake with cream cheese frosting. Finally I settled on a red velvet cake recipe that had been in my family for three generations, and one I knew Clinton loved—Smith Island Cake.

By the time I finished, it was only a few hours until dawn. I debated the merits of getting a bit of sleep or continuing on. The pork loin needed at least three more hours in the smoker, the cakes were cooling on dozens of racks. I'd made the icing for both and had it in the fridge. Deciding I was too wired up to sleep, I peeled and put ten pounds of potatoes on to boil, then pulled the shredded cabbage out of the fridge and went ahead and made the coleslaw. That done, I rinsed the cooked potato cubes and set them aside to cool.

Carrot ginger puree. Coleslaw. Potato salad. Couscous

with chopped kale and halved cherry tomatoes. My special salsa with home-made tortilla chips. Brisket, pulled pork, fried chicken, grilled salmon, and two enormous prime ribs. Just thinking of it nearly gave me an anxiety attack. I had less than twenty-four hours to get all this together. There was no time to mope over a sexy demon. There was no time to do anything except cook.

I checked the pork loins and pulled them from the smoker. The salmon would be grilled early Saturday before the event, and the prime ribs would go in the oven tonight to slow-cook. The most time-consuming dish on my list was the chicken, but I wanted to wait until later this afternoon to start breading and frying that.

In the meantime, there was one more alpha I needed to prepare a special dessert for, and she was the most important of all. Tink might not be an official alpha of either pack, but as Dallas' new mate, her voice carried a lot of authority in his pack. She liked chocolate. And I knew the perfect thing to create in her honor.

Warming three different styles in double boilers on my stove, I began to ice down the giant marble slab where I made my candies. Then I grabbed a set of truffle molds from under the counter. Using a high-quality set of small paint brushes, I coated the molds in chocolate, then put them in the fridge to cool.

I yawned, finally feeling tired enough to sleep, but I couldn't go to bed now with only half my truffles made. Making a pot of coffee to keep me going, I prepared three different types of cream filling for the truffles. A few cups of coffee later and I'd added the filling to the chilled, chocolate-coated molds, then poured additional chocolate on top to create the candies. They all went back into the fridge.

Even with the coffee, exhaustion was starting to creep over me. I glanced at the clock, realizing I could only squeeze in a three-hour block of sleep before I needed to get to work on the rest of the food. It would have to be enough. I checked on everything I'd prepared, then headed to my bedroom, shedding my clothes as I walked. I don't remember getting into bed, so I'm sure I was out the moment my head hit the pillow.

And thankfully, I slept without any dreams of sexy demons.

CHAPTER 19

GLENDA

I maneuvered my van up the steep mountain road, taking care to avoid any ruts or bumps that might disrupt the carefully packed food that filled the entire back of my vehicle. I was operating on that three-hour nap, then another three hours last night. Thankfully a pot of good coffee had revived me in time to finish the chicken, grill the salmon, and get everything loaded. This was a huge catering job for me. It wasn't the largest or the most complex I'd ever pulled off, but it was the most important. The peace between the werewolf packs and their integration into Accident was a pivotal point in our town's history. This barbeque cemented what was to be the "new" Accident, the "new" werewolf culture, our future.

And, of course, there was that little matter of the brisket contest and my soul.

The barbeque was to be held in the area of Heartbreak Mountain that Dallas had gifted as public land for all werewolves regardless of pack affiliation or status. The rules were that none could live there, and that applications for use

"This peace is more important than Dallas or Clinton realize," a voice behind me chimed in. "Werewolves need to embrace the future."

I turned to face Tink. "And the future for werewolves is…?"

"Collaboration with other supernaturals, even though we continue to honor our customs and history. Respect for those wolves who choose to live outside the pack, or even among the humans. Overcoming our terror of the world outside the wards and learning that there are human things to be admired and enjoyed. Step one is for our two packs to be approachable and welcoming to each other."

Basically the same thing we witches wanted. Clearly Tink would be a valuable ally going forward.

"Well, this ice sculpture is beautiful, and I'm sure both it and the barbeque will help with step one."

Tink folded her arms across her chest and looked around with an air of satisfaction. "Everything looks amazing. Back to work everyone! I'll just snag a piece of this fried chicken you're putting out and be back with Dallas later."

She left and Desiree finished with the decorations and drove back with the minotaurs, promising to come by after the event finished to clean everything up. That left me alone, firing up the smoker, prepping the chaffing dishes, and beginning to set out the food. I could hear Lucien's SUV coming up the road. Good. They could help me get the rest of the food out. The guests would begin to arrive any minute. Eating and socializing was the focus of the party, and I wanted to make sure the buffet line was ready when the first hungry attendee arrived.

Pulling one of the bowls of coleslaw from the portable fridge, I turned and nearly dropped it when I saw Xavier standing right behind me.

"Where's your brisket?" It was a stupid thing to ask, but

he had no vehicle, no chafing dish, no serving tray, nothing. Just a devilishly handsome demon standing in a field behind my van.

His smile was wickedly delicious. "Oh, don't worry. I'll have it here in time for the contest." Before I could reply he'd taken the bowl of coleslaw from my hands and carried it to the buffet table. "Here?"

I nodded, my chest aching at how much I missed him. My former resolve began to melt away. The heart wants what the heart wants.

But love couldn't grow on a foundation of distrust. And I wasn't sure I wanted him handling that coleslaw knowing how he'd basically poisoned my slugs.

I marched over and snatched the coleslaw bowl out of his hands, putting it in a completely different place than I'd intended. "Get out, Xavier. You're not invited. You can show up for the contest, then leave directly afterward. You're not welcome here—either at this party, or at my house."

"I just want to talk to you for five damned minutes," he exploded, picking up the coleslaw and moving it to the exact spot I'd wanted it to be. "Five minutes. At least give me that, Glenda."

I sucked in a breath, then counted to ten as I let it out. I still cared about this demon. Just his presence made my heart stutter, my legs tremble, my whole body go warm. And that made me just as mad as what he'd done to the slugs.

At the end of the day, I needed to put this behind me. We might never be lovers or even friends again, but there might be occasions when I'd see him at Cassie's talking to Lucien, or out and about as he did his crossroads demon business. And if he won this little bet of ours and ended up with my soul, maybe it would be a good thing if I at least showed him I was willing to listen to him for five minutes.

"Okay."

He ran a hand through his hair, making it stand up in little spiky bits here and there. "I know you're mad about what I do and who I am. There are limits in my ability to change that. I'm a crossroads demon, and besides that I'm a demon. Certain things are part of my job description. But if you tell me what's acceptable and not to you, I'll honor those limits."

"How about we start with *don't mess with my food*?" I shot back, my intentions of being nice and listening going right out the window.

He shot me a puzzled look. "Okay. That one's easy. I don't mess with your food. Next?"

"I'm serious." It took a concerted effort not to punch him. "I've worked hard to build up a reputation, and I'm very proud of my creations. I know pride is a sin and all that, but sabotaging my food, whether it's for a client or not, isn't something I'm going to forgive."

"I would never do that." He scowled. "If I messed something up while helping you in the kitchen, I can assure you it wasn't intentional."

I hesitated, a horrible feeling coming over me. What if it had been an honest mistake? I'd had him doing the slug prep, as well as the sauce. What if he'd accidently grabbed the wrong spice container? Just because he could make a heck of a tasty sandwich didn't mean he could tell coriander from cardamom.

"I know demons lie, but I need you to tell me the absolute truth here. Did you intentionally add something to the slugs or the sauce that would make the gnomes sick?"

Now he looked rather pissed. "No! I've never cooked slugs before. I did what you told me to do. I would certainly never intentionally do something that would jeopardize your career. In case you didn't notice, Glenda, I like you. I more than like you. I want to spend time with you in the kitchen, in bed, in all sorts of other places. Why in the hell do you think I'd do something that would be guaranteed to make you never want to see me again?"

He was right. I felt like such an idiot. I'd been so afraid of letting myself be vulnerable, about caring and risking my heart, that I'd jumped at the first chance to slam the door on the demon who might be the love of my life. I got scared—scared of my own feelings, scared of my past repeating itself. And I'd made assumptions about him as a demon, and in particular about him as a crossroads demon. My sisters had found love with demons. I would never doubt Lucien's, Hadur's, Nash's, or Eshu's love and dedication to my sisters. Why did I immediately assume the worst of Xavier?

"I'm…I'm sorry." I took a deep breath and prepared to be vulnerable once more, to take a chance on love, on this demon. "I should have talked to you and not just lost my temper and thrown you out. I was embarrassed and humiliated, and I made some horrible assumptions about you."

His eyes searched mine. "So this isn't about what I do as a crossroads demon? You weren't mad at me because you thought I was out all day trading favors for people's souls? That I was taking advantage of every loophole in each of my contracts?"

I shook my head.

"Instead you were mad because something had gone wrong at your catering job, and you assumed I deliberately tampered with your food to sabotage the event."

It was a statement instead of a question. I winced, but kept eye contact and nodded, trying to be brave and take my lumps.

"I sought you out and flirted with you. I talked about food and life, and spent two days working in a kitchen with you. I had sex with you, spent the night and had breakfast with you in the morning. I told you I'd see you later, that I'd be back and that I wanted more than just one night with you—that I wanted so much more. But in spite of that, you still believed I would deliberately mess with your food to screw up your catering job."

I felt myself go hot. "I'm sorry. I'm not good at this. All my other relationships fell apart because the guy liked my food more than he liked me, or he just wanted a weekend fling. You're this hot, sexy, demon, and I…"

"You couldn't accept the fact that I thought you were a hot, sexy, witch who I love spending time with? Your food is amazing, but it's you I care about, Glenda. You."

Me. He cared about me. And I'd almost screwed this up beyond repair. I might *have* screwed this up beyond repair.

"Can you forgive me?"

He stared at me for a moment. "Yes, but I need you trust me, or at least talk to me if you're angry. You can't shut me out like that. I'd thought you were mad about something completely different. I even went to Lucien for help."

My eyes widened. "You went to Lucien and Cassie?" She'd never said one word of this to me, darn her.

"Just Lucien. We spoke in private. Honestly he wasn't all that much help."

The last was said with a wry grin. I thought what I might do if Lucien had come to me to beg Xavier's case for him.

"I wouldn't have backed down for Lucien," I told him. "Cassie, yes. Lucien, no."

"I didn't want him to intervene, just to give me some pointers on how to pacify an angry witch."

I felt myself blush. "I'm not sure I want to know what he said."

Xavier chuckled. "It was basically 'do whatever she says'."

I grinned because that was pretty much the summary of the demon's relationship with my eldest sister.

"So...are we friends?" My face was even hotter. Friends? Lovers? What *was* I supposed to call this thing between us?

He took my hand and shook it, a solemn expression on his face. "Friends. But don't think I'm letting you out of this bet we have going. I didn't slave over this brisket recipe for nothing, you know."

I sucked in an alarmed breath. "No! There's no need to do that. Let's call the bet off."

His eyes narrowed. "Afraid you might lose?"

I bit back an instinctive denial and realized I was. I was still doubting him, worrying what he might demand if he won our bet. But if this fragile relationship would have any chance at survival, I'd need to trust—both him *and* myself.

I sniffed. "Hardly. I just don't want you to embarrass yourself in front of my friends and family. I mean, your slugs had the gnomes all puking. Who knows what your brisket will do to a bunch of werewolves?"

He pointed a finger at me in mock anger. "Those slugs were not my fault. You probably got a batch of expired ones or something. Besides, I don't know how to make sautéed slugs, or whatever, but I do know how to make an amazing brisket."

I lifted my chin. "We'll see. Just don't come crying and begging to me when you lose. Actually, *do* come crying and begging to me. I might like that sort of thing."

"Demons do not beg," he told me in a lofty tone. "Well, except for Lucien."

I barked out a laugh and slapped a hand over my mouth, looking over to see Cassie and Lucien climbing out of the SUV. They were both watching me, Cassie with concern on her face and Lucien poised and ready to no doubt run to my rescue. I gave them a subtle thumbs-up sign and turned back to Xavier.

We were good. We were so good. And I was nearly giddy with joy. I still had the gnomes to pacify, two lone werewolves to help safeguard, and a barbeque contest to win, but things were better than they'd ever been.

CHAPTER 20

GLENDA

"And what exactly was that about?" Cassie stood in front of me, her hands on her hips. "Is that the guy Lucien told me about? The one who messed with your slugs?"

"Wow, he *is* hot," Adrienne exclaimed. Addy and her vulture had arrived just after Lucien and Cassie, and just before Xavier had left in some demon-teleport way that I'd never seen the others besides Eshu use.

"So judging by what I saw of the pair of you, all is forgiven?" Cassie's eyes narrowed. "He screwed with your cooking, and you actually *forgave* him?"

I nodded. "We talked. He swears he didn't do anything intentionally. It must have been a mistake. I *did* have him do the marinade and the sauce for the slugs, and really didn't give adequate supervision."

"Well, I'm glad that's cleared up," Lucien announced cheerfully. "Now he won't take your soul if he somehow manages to win this cooking contest you got yourself mixed up in."

"What?" Cassie shrieked. "Oh Glenda, how could you?"

"Sex," Adrienne told her. "Lots of good sex. It makes *me* agree to all sorts of stupid shit. Can't blame Glenda for that one."

The vulture hissed and bounced his head in agreement.

"It's not like she's going to lose," Lucien reassured Cassie. "This is Glenda we're talking about. Everything she makes is amazing."

"Except for her smoothies," Adrienne added.

"I'm not using healing magic on the brisket, so I think we're okay there," I told her. "Now help me set this stuff out. Dallas, Clinton, and Tink just arrived and the other werewolves won't be far behind them."

Cassie and Lucien headed over to greet the alphas, slackers that they were, but Adrienne stayed to help unload the food and make sure all the canisters for the chafing dishes were lit.

"I'm happy things are working out for you and this demon, Glenda," she said as she stole a piece of pulled pork from a tray and tossed it to the vulture. "I gotta admit that I was kinda psyched about giving him a horrible case of lice though. And having birds poop on his head. You have no idea how much Drake can poop. No one wants that on their head."

"I'm sure there will be another opportunity," I said as I handed her a tray of potato salad.

"Oh, I know. It's just that the party would have been so much more fun if I'd been able to give a demon lice."

I shook my head and smiled at Addy's weirdness, but cars, trucks, and wolves were beginning to arrive and I needed to concentrate on the party.

Dallas, Tink, and Clinton had positioned themselves near the entrance as a receiving party, each of them welcoming werewolves from either pack and people from the town. As everyone streamed in, they made a beeline straight for the buffet, and Addy and I struggled to keep up with refreshing the trays of quickly vanishing food. I rolled my neck to try to release the tension. Everything was going smoothly so far. Yes, the greetings were a bit warmer between pack members and their own alpha, but not so noticeable than anyone might feel slighted. Werewolf politics weren't terribly convoluted, but there were a lot of emphasis on social interactions, so this event was critical in keeping the peace between the two groups.

The clearing was filling up, and everyone was eating—an activity which tended to calm any shifter and especially werewolves. As bellies began to fill and conversation rose to a happy buzz, Alberta and Shelby arrived.

That tension between my shoulders was back with a vengeance. Those closest to the entrance were suddenly silent, and like a wave, the rest of the guests quieted as well. I heard a growl from my left and hoped that Cassie was ready to intervene if necessary. It wasn't like I could do anything other than throw a healing potion into someone's face or stab them with a serving fork.

"Welcome." Dallas' voice sounded like he'd gargled with glass, but he did extend a hand to shake Shelby's. I saw Alberta's aura flare red-gold, the strength of her magic nearly blinding me. Fae were far more powerful than anyone in Accident realized, and although none of the others would ever admit it, trolls had more magic than six fairies combined. I saw Alberta put a protective arm around Shelby's shoulder, then reach forward to shake Dallas' hand. A few more werewolves in the crowd growled.

Tink was the one who broke the tension.

"Shelby!" The diminutive werewolf sprang forward to grab the lone wolf in a hug. "Damn, I've missed you girl! Is Alberta treating you right?" Tink waved a finger at the troll and smiled. "You know I've got your back if she's not being a proper mate to you, Shelby."

Linking her arms with the other werewolf and the troll, Tink paused just a moment for Clinton to greet the two, then proceeded to drag them both over to the buffet. The entire time she loudly exclaimed about how adorable both their outfits were and demanded to know what nail polish Alberta had on.

"Don't got nail polish on," the troll replied, looking rather stunned at the entire turn of events. Her aura had faded into a pleasant lavender and peach hue, so I rolled my neck once more and turned to check the smoker, confident that Tink had everything well in hand.

The new batch of grilled salmon to replace the nearly empty chafing dishes was coming along nicely, and the fifth round of pork loin was ready to coat with my special vinegar-based sauce. The brisket, my pièce de résistance, was nearly done. I'd marinated. I'd dry rubbed. I'd smoked. This baby was gonna be amazing, and it was going to beat the pants off Xavier's or I wasn't a witch with an incredible talent in the kitchen.

Mmmm. Xavier without pants. The very idea made my legs weak. Would we jump right back into bed tonight, picking up where we'd left off after I'd had my freak-out, or would we take it slow and actually court and woo each other for a while? I hoped for the former, because I was a witch with very little patience, and now that I'd decided to trust him, my heart was racing forward at the speed of sound.

I filled a metal chafing dish with the grilled salmon and headed to refill the buffet line just as Tink, Alberta, and Shelby started to fill their plates.

"Hi Glenda!" Shelby's voice was high and nervous, the whites of her eyes showing clear around the dark brown irises. "How did those spices and herbs work out? It was good to see you last week. You need to come over more often for tea, or whisky, or a rare steak."

Her aura flared with anxiety, and I wanted to give her a hug. Shelby was a bad-ass werewolf who could take on just about anyone in her former pack and come out on top, but she was clearly uneasy about her place now that she was a lone wolf who'd left the pack to mate with a troll.

"I'd love to come by for tea and a rare steak sometime," I told her. "The gnome party didn't work out all that well, but I'm sure the herbs and spices you both supplied were amazing as always. A new assistant of mine accidently put some coriander into the slug marinade and gnomes don't do well with coriander."

Alberta recoiled, her eyes wide. "Coriander?"

I nodded and gave her an apologetic smile. "I know. I must have had a jar on the counter next to your herbs and spices, and my assistant didn't know not to include it. I'll just need to be more careful in the future and make sure my instructions are very detailed."

"Shit. Shit!" Alberta turned to Shelby and said something rapidly in fae. Shelby replied and I found myself wondering when the werewolf had learned the troll's language.

Shelby paled. "Oh no! Glenda, I am so sorry! This is all my fault. What can I do to make things right? It's all my fault."

I shook my head. "What are you talking about?"

"She gave you the wrong bag of herbs and spices," Alberta said. "You were supposed to get the other bag, and the centaurs were supposed to get the one you received. I would never have included coriander in an herbal mixture that was intended for gnome food. I know better than that."

"It was all my fault." Tears sparkled in Shelby's eyes. "I didn't know anything of herbs or spices before I moved in with Alberta. Werewolves aren't sensitive to anything beyond wolf's bane and a few other herbs, so I didn't even notice. I've got no idea what makes gnomes sick or makes merfolk sick or makes fae sick beyond what Alberta gets green over. I'm so sorry."

I reached over the buffet trays to grab her hands. "It's not your fault. You didn't know. Honestly it's my fault for not checking the herbs and spices before I used them. I got distracted by...something. And I was hurrying, and using an assistant who wouldn't know the difference. It's completely my fault, not yours."

"I need to label my deliveries better," Alberta said. "And I need to spend more time showing Shelby what's what. I'll talk to the gnomes and explain what happened. I don't want you to take the blame for this one, Glenda."

I'd blamed Xavier for this when the packet of herbs and spices he'd used had been the wrong one. It was completely my fault for not checking it. I'd been busy, distracted by what had happened to Stanley, really distracted by my attraction to Xavier, and I'd not taken proper care to check what I was adding to the slug sauce.

"No, I'm the one who prepared the dish. I'm the one that didn't check the spice mixture. It's my fault, not yours." I smiled at the troll, then at the werewolf. "It's okay. I can see how such a mistake would happen. Coriander is a common spice, and I can't imagine that Shelby would know such a thing would be harmful to gnomes."

"I'll learn more," the werewolf vowed. "And I'll make sure I pay more attention to Alberta's instructions in the future."

"And I'll make sure I label the bags," Alberta added. "If I can do anything in the future to make this up to you, please let me know. I'm so embarrassed that you got the wrong delivery, and I swear this won't ever happen again."

"No worries, Alberta. Mistakes happen, and I'm not going to hold you responsible for this. I know how much pride you take in your gardening." I heaped a huge helping of grilled salmon onto Shelby's plate, knowing how much the were-wolf loved fish, then left the buffet line to return to my smoker.

It hadn't been Xavier's fault at all. Not only had I blamed him for intentionally tampering with the food, but even after our conversation today I'd assumed his unintentional mistake had led to the coriander in the slugs. Come to find out the problem had been in the spice bag I'd gotten from Alberta.

I was such a fool. I'd thrown away a potentially amazing relationship because I'd jumped to conclusions, because I'd let my past baggage weigh heavy on my mind. I owed Xavier an additional apology, and I needed to stop my knee-jerk reactions and actually trust my emotions for once in my freaking life.

I added more pork to the chafing dish, then checked again on the brisket, tearing off a sliver to taste. It was the best I'd ever made. The flavors made my eyes roll back in my head and brought me to the edge of a food orgasm. If Xavier's was better than this, then he was truly my master.

That thought led me down all sorts of naughty pathways. What if he won? What sort of thing would he ask of me? I wasn't worried any more about him demanding my soul, instead I was titillated thinking of kinky stuff he might ask as his reward.

But he'd never win. My brisket was damned good, and although pride might be my sin, I knew good food when I tasted it.

"Stanley's here." Adrienne appeared beside me and snuck a quick grab of brisket. The vulture behind her protested, and she grabbed another piece to toss to him. "Drake likes his meat raw and about two days fermenting in the sun, but he says yours is a close second."

Great. My cooking was a close second to roadkill in the opinion of a vulture. "I don't see Stanley," I said, looking over toward the entrance.

"The flies say he's a hundred yards out, but approaching." Adrienne snagged another piece of brisket. "He's alone."

Alone. Bart hadn't come with him. I had mixed feelings about that. I knew Stanley wanted him to lay low, but I'd really hoped that Bart would attend. Actually I hoped that Bart and Stanley would attend together. The fact that Stanley was coming to the barbeque by himself spoke to his courage, and his faith in us witches to protect him. I wasn't about to let him down.

I left Adrienne picking bits of brisket off the smoker and headed to the entranceway where Dallas and Clinton stood. The two alphas, father and son, where chatting in an amicable tone that I'd never imagined would happen a month ago. Tink was off sitting with Alberta and Shelby as they ate, ensuring they both had her visible support as the alpha's mate. But Stanley…

I hung near the entrance as the werewolf came from the forest. I was sure most in the room had smelled him arriving from a mile away given their shifter noses and the prevailing winds, but unlike with Alberta and Shelby, conversation did not halt when Stanley arrived—it continued as if he were invisible.

Dallas greeted him stiffly, shaking his hand and making the bare minimum of welcoming conversation. Clinton did the same. Stanley was tense and nervous as he moved past the alphas into the clearing. I intercepted him, guiding him toward the buffet line.

"Everything okay?"

He nodded. "So far. Ain't seen anyone besides you come to welcome me."

"Bart?" I looked around for the other werewolf.

Stanley bared his teeth. "I'm not gonna risk his status in the pack. Either I can stand on my own or I can't."

Okay then. I glanced over to where Shelby and Alberta and Tink were sitting and chatting, and debated the wisdom of placing Stanley there. I didn't want to segregate the lone wolves, even though Tink seemed to be making it her mission to bring them into the fold. There wasn't anyone else that I could sit Stanley next to other than Petunia, who was his boss at the auto repair, bait, and beer shop. What I really wanted was to begin to integrate him back into the wolf packs, though, and I didn't see how that would be possible.

"Grab some food from the buffet and sit with Petunia or my sisters," I told him, regretting that I couldn't do more.

Stanley nodded and headed off, filling a plate and making his way through the tables. A few werewolves growled. Some put their feet out as if to trip him. Others scoffed, and I heard the word "traitor" bandied about. I held my breath, wondering what the heck I'd do if someone tried to attack the werewolf.

That was Cassie's job. And Bronwyn's. My witch siblings who could do more than make nasty tasting potions that healed people. All I could do was watch and hope for the best.

Stanley sat down with Petunia and his crew, and I turned my attention back to the buffet. There was a hectic few hours of refilling meat and the other chafing dishes as everyone ate. A group of werewolves took the stage with instruments to start some folk tunes, and several couples got up to dance. Dallas and Clinton had moved from the entrance to get their own plates of food, and I was happy to see the pair sit down next to each other and enjoy some friendly conversation as they ate. Once again the tension between my shoulders relaxed and I hoped that this would be the event that solidified peace between the werewolf packs, and provided a link between them and the other supernatural creatures in town including the lone wolves.

Finally the moment came and Dallas, Tink, and Clinton rose to announce the contest. There were lengthy speeches on both side about packs, loyalty, and solidarity, then they joked about their prowess in deciding the best brisket at the barbeque. I looked across the clearing, and for the first time in hours saw Xavier smiling with a smug expression as he held a platter of meat in front of him.

I pulled mine from the smoker and sliced it as I watched the demon present his brisket. Dallas, Clinton, and Tink all took a substantial helping, making approving noises as they ate.

It would really suck to lose out to Xavier on a matter of cooking. The nervousness I'd felt over him dragging me off to hell or taking my soul as his reward had vanished, and now I only pondered what a sting to my pride a loss would be. My cooking had always been the best ever since I'd been a child. To have someone else's food judged superior would truly wound.

But maybe there was room in the world, and in Accident, for two amazing chefs. Xavier might beat me out on brisket, but I knew I still held the crown when it came to baked goods. Perhaps sharing the honor of best chef would be a good thing. I could feature some of his dishes in my catering jobs. He might eventually become a partner in my business with specialties of his own. And how nice would it be to relax for once and let someone else cook for me?

I swirled my special cognac sauce on the bottom of a platter, layered my brisket slices on top, then sprinkled on some fresh cracked peppercorn. With a quick wipe to make sure the serving dish was pristine, I made my way over to where the alphas sat.

"Gonna be hard to beat this one, Glenda." Clinton stabbed

another slice from Xavier's nearly empty tray and shoved it in his mouth.

"Thinking we need to make him an honorary werewolf," Dallas said as I moved Xavier's tray to the side and put my platter in front of the three werewolves.

They all seemed happy, joking with each other and sitting together like this. The barbeque had been a success. Everywhere werewolves were mingling with other townsfolk, and the two packs were slowly starting to socialize with each other, migrating into mixed groups. This was what my sisters and I wanted—two packs living in harmony with the rest of the town. No more werewolf isolation. No more violence in the mountains between the two groups. Yes, they'd probably always live apart from the rest of Accident, but we'd all benefit if the us-versus-them mentality vanished.

"I'd love to be an honorary werewolf," Xavier replied to Dallas. "All it will cost you is your soul."

"I don't think that's what he meant." I playfully swatted Xavier on the shoulder. "And souls inside the wards are off limits, demon. Make your deals outside of Accident."

This was fun. This was amazingly fun. All of us here joking and enjoying the food and the friendship. And Xavier by my side, my…friend. More than a friend.

"Changing the rules are we?" The crossroads demon wiggled his eyebrows at me. "I'll honor this new mandate, but rules put in place after a bet is made don't apply. If I win this contest, I get anything I want. There were no limitations at the time of our bargain."

I saw Cassie's aura flare bright white, saw the determination in her face. She'd be there to help me if I needed it, but I didn't need her help.

Trust. We'd never have anything together if I couldn't trust him.

I rolled my eyes. "Like you'd want my soul. Two hours and you'd be begging me to take it back."

He chuckled. "You're probably right. But quit stalling. Serve your meat and get ready for defeat."

I bit back a laugh at the rhyme and scooped the slices of brisket from my platter onto fresh plates.

The werewolves dug in, and the only sound for the next few minutes was the scrape of knives on the plates. Tink was the first to say something.

"Damn, girl. I think I came in my pants just now." She sat back and licked the sauce off her fork. "Forget making that demon an honorary werewolf. I want you to come up to the compound and cook for me every day. I'd be so fat they'd need to wheel me through the woods in a cart for our hunts. Honey, can we afford to hire Glenda as our personal alpha-house chef?"

"Mrmfrm," Dallas responded, not even looking at her as he chewed.

"I thought Bart's smoked trout was good." Clinton shook his head, then shoved another piece of brisket in his mouth. "Mmmm. Mmmm, mmmm."

"Almost as good as raw venison straight from the kill," Dallas finally said. "And that's saying something. Thought that ginger cake of yours was good, Glenda, but this here is a clear winner. You got my vote."

I couldn't help but grin and do a little hop-dance in excitement.

"Glenda gets my vote, too." Dallas raised his fork in the air as he spoke, as if he were royalty making a proclamation.

"Mine too. And I still want to hire you full time." Tink winked at me. "Or at least get on your catering schedule for the harvest party if you're available."

"I'm calling a foul. Clearly the witch paid the three of you off. There's no way her brisket is better than mine." Xavier reached past me, picking up a slice of brisket off the platter with his fingers dripping sauce down his hands and chin as he shoved it into his mouth. When he was done with the piece, he licked the sauce off his hand and winked at me.

"I might be a demon, but I cannot lie when it comes to food. Glenda, once more I bow before you and declare you the master of all things food."

The crowd cheered. Tink clapped her hands. "What are you going to ask him for, Glenda? You won, and now he has to give you anything you want."

I was pretty sure I was more red than the rarest prime rib right now. Tink was looking at me. My sisters were looking at me. *Everyone* was looking at me.

Xavier folded his arms across his chest, that little smirk on his face. "Yes, Glenda the Good Witch, what do you ask of me? I'm bound by my promise to give you anything."

I was about to die of embarrassment right now.

"I've got some suggestions!" Sylvie called out.

"Which means they're X-rated, of course," Bronwyn chimed in.

X-rated suggestions were the last thing I wanted to hear —well out here in public anyway. With all sorts of naughty ideas racing through my mind, I blurted out "pizza oven".

"What?" Tink tilted her head and stared at me.

"I want a Mugnaini wood-fired pizza oven."

"Color me shocked," Cassie drawled.

"My money was on one of those zucchini spiralizers," Ophelia added.

Xavier performed a stately bow before me. "Your wish is my command. If the witch wants a pizza oven, then that's what she'll get."

"Wood-fired," I reminded him, hoping he understood the subtext. "Mugnaini, because it's the best."

"And only the best will do for my witch." He turned about

and walked away, into the forest and out of sight. I watched him go, not quite sure what had just happened. Did he understand that it was *him* I wanted, not a pizza oven? We'd been using that as a euphemism for sex since we'd had the sandwich contest. Surely he couldn't have forgotten.

Maybe he was going to my house to wait for me, naked and in my bed? I hoped so, although he'd have quite a wait because the barbeque wasn't over yet, and I still had a lot of clean up and put away before I headed home.

"I thought you said everything was okay between the pair of you?" Adrienne stepped up beside me and put an arm around my shoulders.

"It is." I looked in the direction Xavier had gone.

"Then what's with the pizza oven? And why did he leave?"

"He should have stayed and helped you clean up," Babylon added, walking up to my other side. "Just like a man to eat and leave you holding an entire buffet full of dirty dishes."

"You'll have to train him," Cassie said from behind me. "Trust me, it's a lifelong process."

"But in the meantime, we'll help you clean up." Bronwyn said.

"Absolutely," Ophelia added.

"I'll help too, although I can think of a lot better things to ask a hot demon to do for me than getting me a lousy pizza oven." Sylvie laughed, then led the way.

CHAPTER 21

GLENDA

y sisters tackled the buffet leftovers, while I put out the cakes, pies, and chocolates along with little signs identifying them and their special significance to each alpha. They were a huge hit, and I heard several werewolves from different packs joking about whether they were a "Dallas pie wolf" or a "Clinton cake wolf". The truffles I'd made in honor of Tink went even faster than the cakes and pies, so I bagged a couple and put them into the pocket of my baggy work pants to take home for Xavier to try.

Only a few hours more, and I'd be home. And for once in my adult life I was going to let all these dirty pans and dishes stay in the van until morning. All I wanted was to see Xavier, to spend some time in his arms. And none of my romantic fantasies included scrubbing pots and pans.

Tink once more made her way to Shelby and Alberta, talking animatedly with the pair of them, and grabbing another werewolf to include in their conversation. I turned to look for Stanley, but didn't see him. Had he gone home? He'd been over by Petunia just a few minutes ago eating a piece of cake. I knew he felt awkward and unwanted here, and I wouldn't blame him for sneaking off unnoticed. It made me feel bad that I hadn't had time to sit with him and at least give him someone to talk to besides a few of the town folk and his boss. Clinton and Dallas hadn't exactly been warm and fuzzy to the other werewolf, but they *had* welcomed him and shook his hand. That should have been enough to at least keep him from being snubbed.

But it still had to have been awkward and lonely being surrounded by former pack mates who wouldn't even speak to him.

Worried, I made my way to Petunia, taking the boar shifter a second piece of caramel apple pie.

"Thank you, Glenda." He took the pie with a smile. "The food today was real good. I especially liked the fried chicken."

"If there's any leftover, I'll bring some by the shop tomorrow." I looked around again. "Did Stanley leave? I saw him sitting next to you earlier."

The boar shifter nodded. "That poor guy can't catch a break. I know how lonely he gets without his kinfolk around. Me and the other shifters aren't the same as having wolves to pal around with, especially since he was raised pretty much only knowing werewolves until his teens. I was glad when that wolf came and told him his friend was here and wanted to see him."

"Bart?" I looked around, but didn't see either of the werewolves.

"Yeah, Bart. That wolf delivering the message didn't look too happy about it. I know the pair of them have been keeping it quiet that they're hanging out together. Stanley told me he made Bart promise not to come to the barbeque, or if he did, not to talk to him. He doesn't want his friend to be going through the same kind of shunning." Petunia shook his head. "Don't understand it all. Boars don't do that kind of thing, but then again we don't live in packs either. Just couples and young. Sometimes family gets together for holidays, but most of the time we're living alone until we find a mate. I try to be sympathetic, but it's hard to understand when Stanley gets mopey."

"But Bart told someone? Another werewolf?" None of this made sense, and a chill was beginning to shiver its way down my spine. The two of them had been so careful, and outside of my sisters and I, and Petunia, no one else knew that Bart had remained friends with Stanley after his exile. Had they been discovered? Had someone followed Bart and seen him pick Stanley up from the hospital? Seen him at Stanley's house the other night?

"What did this werewolf look like?"

Petunia scratched his chin. "They kinda all look the same, you know? Brown hair. Not a lot of beard. I'm assuming it was a female because she had her nails painted real nice. Corvette red."

I immediately envisioned bright red nails. Red polish. Like red paint. Polish that could have dripped onto a hiking boot and stayed there, a crimson blob on the brown leather. With a hasty good-bye, I left Petunia and ran to where I'd last seen the alphas. Dallas and Clinton were talking to a group of fairies. Without even an apology, I barged right into the middle of them and interrupted a conversation about power tools.

"Is Bart here?" I asked Dallas. "Did he come today? Has anyone seen him?"

I was in near panic, but I didn't want to make a complete fool of myself and risk exposing Bart and Stanley if I was wrong.

"No. He said he was going fishing." Dallas shrugged. "Normally I would have insisted he come along and at least stay for an hour, but I know how close he and Stanley were, and I figured he just couldn't bear to see him yet. I'm hoping he'll come around soon, but it will take time."

I tried to steady my breathing. Werewolves were notorious gossips. If one of them had discovered that Bart was sneaking into town to see Stanley, then the entire compound would have known about it—Dallas would have definitely known about it. And the only reason someone would have for keeping such a juicy tidbit of gossip to themselves would be if they had another use for it.

Like to use the information to lure Stanley off into the woods by himself, where he would be unsuspectingly set upon and injured. Killed.

"Who wears red nail polish?" I looked back and forth between Clinton and Dallas.

"I do," one of the fairies chimed in unhelpfully.

"A werewolf," I added breathlessly. "What female werewolf with a beard and brown hair wears bright red nail polish?"

Dallas and Clinton exchanged puzzled looks. "Don't pay much attention to what nail color a woman's got on," the elder alpha said.

Crap. There was one werewolf who might have paid attention, a werewolf alpha who loved make-up and a good mani-pedi. I left Dallas and Clinton just as abruptly as I'd arrived and raced over to where Tink was chatting with Adrienne and Ophelia.

"I need you to see if you can divine where Stanley is," I told Ophelia.

Her eyes widened. "He's gone? You don't think…"

"Stanley?" Tink shrugged. "Maybe he went home? I was meaning to go over and talk to him, but by the time I finished forcing a couple of my packmates to talk to Alberta and Shelby, I couldn't find him."

"Petunia said a werewolf came and told him to meet…

meet someone in the woods. Brown hair. Brown beard. Bright red nail polish."

"Oh, that's nice," Tink said. "I'm glad someone is reaching out to him."

I threw up my hands in exasperation. "It's not nice. That someone is trying to kill him. A werewolf tampered with Stanley's car last weekend, then followed him and kicked the jack out when Stanley was under it. If I hadn't come by, he might not have made it. This werewolf with the red nails lured him into the woods, and I think she's the one who tried to kill him before. I need to know what female in your pack likes to wear bright red nail polish."

I knew none of that probably made much sense, but I didn't have time to explain it all to Tink in detail.

"Well, me, but obviously it's not me." Tink held up her hands. "I only do red in the fall and winter. Summer is for corals and fun colors like lavender and lime green. Unless you've got a formal event and a red dress, but even then I'm not a fan of the matchy-matchy stuff."

"Tink!" I curled my hands into fists to keep from shaking her. Shaking one of the pack alphas wouldn't be a good thing. "Who else? We need to know."

She pursed her lips and tapped them with a manicured coral fingernail. "I remember Briarly always has her nails red. Says it reminds her of blood after the hunt. She's romantic that way."

"Briarly?" I wracked my brain trying to remember if I'd ever met her.

"She's Bart's sister. She never liked Stanley, but I can't think why she'd be going after him now. I mean, she should be happy about his exile. She hated that they were always together, fishing and hunting, and watching those survival shows, drinking beer down at Pistol Pete's. But since Stanley was exiled, Bart won't even mention his name. Bart's loyal, and Stanley's betrayal hurt him deep. There's no reason for Briarly to want Stanley hurt or dead. Not now, anyway."

"Crap," Ophelia muttered. "Stupid Mercury retrograde. I can't get a fix on him. All I see is forest, and red, and something that looks like a rock."

I ground my teeth in frustration. We had a name, but that wouldn't do us any good if we couldn't get to Stanley in time. Was he hurt? Was he already dead? His safety mattered far more to me right now that delivering justice to this Briarly wolf.

Although that was a strong second on my to-do list.

"Can you track him? Or her?" I asked Tink. "Is there any way you can lead us to Stanley? Or if not him, to this Briarly?"

"I'll do my best to pick up a scent."

Tink headed to the perimeter of the clearing where we were holding the party and began weaving her way back and forth among the trees and bushes, her mouth slightly open as she breathed in. Adrienne and I followed her while Ophelia went to get Cassie and Lucien, and to alert the other alphas. As we moved, I noticed Addy brushing her hand across bushes Tink had already sniffed and murmuring something.

"Mobilizing my insect friends," she said at my questioning glance. "Insects use odor signals to communicate with each other, and their ability to detect these scents over distances as long as several miles is great. I've asked them to notify me of 'food' that came out of the clearing and headed into the woods."

"Flies see us as food?" Ugh, that was so disgusting. We'd used Addy on occasion to keep ants away from our picnic baskets, but I'd never considered that bugs might be as interested in us as in our lunches.

"They don't see us as food—well, unless we're dead because then we're food for everyone. Flies see us more as the food delivery guys. We eat meat and they eat meat. We sometimes have food residue on our clothing and skin. Our sweat and breath often smells of last night's dinner. They're not dumb. They know if they smell a human, or in this case a werewolf, that dinner is most likely nearby."

Disgusting, but intriguing. "What about fairies?"

Adrienne knelt down to put her hand beside an ant's mound before responding. "Insects don't like fae. Well, except for trolls. From what a few flies have told me, fae smell bad. I think it's a lavender odor, but I don't know if it's intentional on their part, or part of their natural scent."

"But trolls?" I was definitely intrigued.

"Trolls evidently can change their scent pattern. Their glamour abilities are the highest of the fae, and since they enjoy gardening, they take care not to offend or repel useful insects. They like to blend into their surroundings, and mesh with the circle of life, so their scent changes from neutral to whatever balances best with their current environment."

"I've got it!" Tink cried out, cutting off any further conversation on insects and fae odor.

Tink took off and Adrienne and I ran after her, struggling not to lose sight of the werewolf as she barreled through the forest. Just as she vanished out of sight, I heard a snarl that sent shivers down my back, followed by a ripping sound.

Adrienne and I burst into a rocky clearing just in time to see Tink launch herself at a werewolf in human form. The werewolf cowered before her alpha, but survival instinct overruled pack hierarchy, and in a flash the two wolves were rolling across the ground, snapping at each other. The wolf that I assumed was Briarly managed to roll free and tried to run for the woods, only to be tackled by Tink within a few strides.

Tink was a tiny werewolf in her human form, and she wasn't as large as the other werewolf in her animal form, but the alpha was fierce and fast. Still, the other werewolf was steadily overpowering her as they rolled and bit. Knowing I'd only end up hurt if I got in the middle of the fight and tried to help, I turned away from Tink and looked for Stanley.

The other werewolf wasn't in the clearing, so I headed to where I'd seen Briarly standing when Tink had first jumped her. Climbing a pile of rocks, I pushed myself up and onto a flat boulder and nearly fell off the other side where a sheer drop of twenty feet ended with a narrow shelf and a tree growing sideways from the rockface.

Hanging half on the tree and half on the ledge was an unconscious and bleeding Stanley.

"Get Cassie," I shouted back to Adrienne.

There was no way I could get the werewolf up off that ledge unassisted, but there might be a way I could get down to him. Taking a steadying breath, I studied the cliff side, and tried to remember all the years I'd climbed this mountain as a kid, all the times I'd clawed my way up a rockface with tiny handholds and not much to support my weight.

All the times I'd almost fallen but been too young to realize the consequences of such a fall. Kids feel invincible. A twenty-seven-year-old woman does not feel so invincible, and eyeing the descent, all I could think of was my body splatted below in a twisted heap of broken bones and flesh.

But something tugged at me deep inside where my magic dwelled. Something told me that Stanley needed me. I was a witch who had no offensive or defensive capabilities. I was shit in a fight, but I could heal, and right now I knew that's what Stanley needed.

Gritting my teeth, I lowered myself over the edge, envisioning the path I needed to take to safely get down to where Stanley was. The muscles in my arms trembled as I gingerly felt for toe-holds to support my weight.

One rock slipped under my foot, sending the stone clattering down the side of the mountain, but my other foot found a stable hold, and the next rock helped balance my weight. Relaxing for a moment, I eased one hand down, testing my weight on the rock before lowering the opposing foot to a thick root extending from a crack in a sheer space of stone.

Slowly I made my way down until I found myself on the narrow ledge with Stanley. Forcing myself not to immediately provide aid to the werewolf, I took in my surroundings. The tree where Stanley's legs were tangled was anchored deep in the cliff face, and there were several smaller trees just like it a few feet below the werewolf. The shelf where I stood and where Stanley's upper body rested was narrow, but widened off to my right. A stout bush jutted out just where the ledge ended.

The hearty trees and shrubs gave me something to quickly grab if I started to slip off the shelf. But I wasn't the problem right now, it was Stanley. If I slid him off the tree to lay down on the ledge, his weight might pull the pair of us off the side. And there was no way I could hold Stanley's weight *and* catch myself on the trees.

Lowering myself to the ledge, I eased forward toward Stanley and put my fingers on his neck. His pulse was slow and thready. There was blood from a head wound, and from a bunch of scratches, and his one leg twisted at an abnormal angle. But aside from that, he didn't seem to be suffering from any significant injury.

Why was he unconscious? I'd seen werewolves not even notice these types of injuries. I ran my hands over his face and dark brown beard, then down his neck to his chest, closing my eyes as I tried to sense where unseen injuries might be.

It hit me with a strength that made my nose twitch and

eyes sting. I sneezed, then pulled my hands away to rub my eyes.

Wolfsbane. A *lot* of wolfsbane.

It caused an allergic reaction among werewolves, but just like allergies in humans, their reactions and sensitivity varied. Most werewolves got itchy hives. Some couldn't shift for a few hours. Some had reduced abilities to heal. Some had life-threatening incidents of anaphylactic shock.

I wasn't an expert in werewolf culture, but I knew that physical weaknesses were considered character flaws among them. Physical strength, the ability to quickly heal wounds, and a stoic endurance of any pain—physical or emotional— was highly prized. Ophelia and I had spent hours discussing how frustrating this was, and how it hindered our ability to help werewolf patients who weren't forthcoming about aller-gies, sensitivities, past injuries, or genetic conditions.

Clearly this level of wolfsbane was not only keeping Stanley in an unconscious state and hindering his breathing, but it was also blocking his shifter ability to heal. In his current condition, if he hadn't been caught on this tree and ledge, if he'd fallen all the way down this cliff, then he might have died. Briarly must have somehow dosed him with wolfs-bane without becoming affected herself, then tossed him over this cliff. When we'd arrived, she was probably trying to figure out how to knock him off the ledge and all the way down.

I heard a yelp from up above and grimaced, hoping Tink was doing okay.

Reaching out to check Stanley's pulse again, I was alarmed at his slowing heartbeat and the shallow breathing. And here I was with nothing to help him. I'd brought healing potions, but in my panic, I'd left them all in the van. All I could do was hope to keep the werewolf stable, and pray that Cassie and Lucien got here soon.

A rock the size of a softball nearly missed my head, hitting Stanley in the abdomen and sliding him toward the edge of the shelf. I grabbed him, and glanced up to see Briarly, aiming another rock at us. Had she bested Tink? She must know that she'd be put to death for killing Dallas' mate and co-alpha of the pack. Was she so desperate to murder Stanley that she'd sacrifice her own life for this?

Another rock hit the tree where Stanley's legs were tangled. It bounced and one of his legs came free, shifting his weight even further off the ledge. I braced myself against the cliff face, looping an arm around the thorny bush and holding onto Stanley's waistband with the other hand.

I had to do something. Cassie was probably on her way, but this werewolf might knock both Stanley and me off the ledge before she got here to help. If only he wasn't unconscious. I could manage myself if I didn't have to worry about holding Stanley's weight.

If only he wasn't unconscious. If only I could clear the effects of the wolfsbane from him, heal him, and wake him up, then he could easily scale up the side of this cliff and fight Briarly while I made my much slower way up. I'd only ever healed with smoothies, mixing my magic with the fruit and yogurt into something magical that tasted like paint and sweaty gym socks. But Xavier had insisted there was magic in all my cooking. Hoping I didn't get hit by a rock, I let go of the bush and reached inside my pocket for a bag holding two truffles.

Another rock bounced off the cliff face above my head, sending a shower of pebbles and dirt down on us. I took the chocolates from the plastic bag, held them in my hand, and poured my magic into them.

A rock hit the tree, and both Stanley's legs came free. I gasped, and nearly dropped the chocolates as I grabbed him with both hands, easing him onto the ledge partially on top of me. Wrapping my arms around him, I gripped the smashed chocolates tightly and again sent my magic into them, trying not to think about how one well-aimed rock would send us both plunging downward.

A rock chipped the corner of the ledge. Time was running out. These crushed, half-melted chocolates in my hand weren't smoothies, but they'd have to do. Another rock barely missed us as I reached over and crammed the chocolates into Stanley's mouth, holding it shut and rubbing his throat as if I were giving a pill to a dog.

Looking up I saw Briarly leaning out over the cliff edge, a huge rock in her hands. This time she was taking careful aim. She held the boulder in both hands and began to raise it over her head, shifting her weight to keep from falling over the edge herself. I gritted my teeth and held Stanley's mouth shut as he choked and gagged on the chocolates.

We weren't going to make it. Well, I wasn't going to make it. This boulder would hit us, sending us both off the edge, and where Stanley might survive thanks to my chocolates, I'd have no such luck.

Fear spiked through me as I watched Briarly, unable to look away. Then something hit her from behind—something that snarled ferociously. The two werewolves tumbled over the cliff, both scrabbling for the trees jutting from the rock-face as they fell.

Stanley began to squirm, and I let go of his mouth. His eyes opened and he sucked in a breath, gagging and spitting as if he might vomit. With a shudder, he partially shifted, his hands and feet becoming claws.

"Don't stab me," I told him. "It would really suck if I survived Briarly only to have my patient claw me to death."

"What...what happened?" Stanley looked around, eyes wide. "Briarly said Bart needed to talk to me—something urgent. Then there was wolfsbane, and that's all I remember."

He shuddered again. "Stuff nearly killed me twenty years ago when a tree branch broke and I felt into a patch of it."

"Briarly threw you over the cliff, but you got caught on the tree and this ledge." I shifted slightly, trying to look over. Were the two werewolves down at the bottom, broken and injured? Or dead? I almost didn't want to look.

But if I hadn't looked, I wouldn't have seen Tink, climbing her way up the rockface, jabbing her claws into the cliff on her way. She was covered in blood, but had a determined expression on her face that reminded me as tiny as she was, she was still one hundred percent the alpha.

"How's your leg?" I asked Stanley, wondering if he'd healed enough that he could make his way up the rocks the same way Tink was.

Stanley grimaced. "Healing, but not to the point I can climb with it. I could just stay here an hour or so, then climb up."

"Nonsense." Tink pulled herself onto the tree next to us that had previously held Stanley's legs. Sometime during the climb she'd shifted back into human form and was both naked and still covered in blood. "You can do it three-legged. Shift into wolf form, and I'll help you up."

Stanley did as she commanded, careful not to crowd me off the ledge. Between the two of them, they both made their way up the rest of the way. I held my breath, nearly having a panic attack each time one of their hands, or paws, slipped, letting it out as they both disappeared over the top.

Now it was my turn.

I was shaky from all the adrenaline, but going up had always been easier for me than climbing down. By the time I heaved myself over the top edge, I was thinking I needed to get back into climbing again. Maybe I could take a look at my schedule and take Tuesday mornings off? I wondered if Xavier liked to climb.

Tink and Stanley helped me to my feet, Stanley gingerly putting weight on the leg that had been broken.

"Thanks for healing me, Glenda. Again." Stanley wrinkled up his nose and shuddered. "Whatever that was you shoved in my mouth, it was worse than your smoothies. It was like eating poop, and not the good kind either."

There were good kinds of poop? I really didn't want to know about that. Instead I patted Stanley on the shoulder, examined Tink for injuries, and joked about making her lick the melted chocolate off my hand to heal her.

"No way," she laughed. "I'll suffer. I don't want to be put off eating chocolate for the rest of my life."

It was then that Cassie, Lucien, Adrienne, Dallas, and Clinton all burst into the clearing.

"Too late, as always," I called out with a smile to let them know we were all okay. My smile must not have been too reassuring because Dallas grabbed Tink in his arms, nearly crushing her, and Cassie immediately began to examine me, asking questions, as she exclaimed over every tiny scratch and minor bruise.

"I had worse when I used to climb as a kid," I told her.

"Yeah, and I about had a heart attack every time you headed up the mountains with your gear. I celebrated the day you gave all that up and decided just to cook instead."

I rolled my eyes, thinking my eldest sister probably still worried about my burning myself on the stove, or slicing a finger chopping vegetables. That's what Cassie did; she worried. And now was definitely not the time to tell her I was thinking of taking up climbing again.

"What'll happen with Briarly?" I heard Stanley ask Dallas and Tink.

I nearly fell over with astonishment when Dallas turned to Cassie. "Assuming the sheriff needs a call on this one?"

Two months ago, the werewolf pack would have handled

it themselves, either by delivering a death sentence or banishing the wolf who'd gone against her alpha's laws.

"Yes, but we'll be taking your input on this one, Dallas," Cassie replied. "I doubt a long prison sentence would be appropriate for a werewolf, and we don't really have the facilities to jail a wolf for a decade or so."

Dallas nodded. "Thinking banishment once she's healed, but I want to hear what Stanley wants to happen."

I turned to the lone wolf, shocked once again that the alpha of the pack was allowing a lone wolf, an exile from their pack, input on appropriate sentencing.

Stanley nodded. "I don't want her dead. She's Bart's sister. I'm thinking exile from Accident with a review every ten years regarding reinstatement?"

"Agreed." Dallas looked down at Tink. "Do you want to coordinate her retrieval and escort her into town to the sheriff's office?"

Tink grinned. "It would be my pleasure."

We all made our way back to the clearing, where the guests had gone leaving only my sisters cleaning up my supplies and loading them into the van. Desiree and her helpers had come back and were making short work of the tables and chairs. The beautiful ice sculpture remained, glistening as it slowly melted in the sun.

The party had been a huge success. Stanley's attacker had been caught and would face justice. Things were changing in Accident for the better.

And I had a boyfriend, who was probably waiting naked for me at home. Grabbing a few empty trays from the buffet table, I shoved them haphazardly in the back of the van. I didn't care what sort of mess I was making. I'd deal with it tomorrow. All I wanted right now was to go home—to go home to my demon.

CHAPTER 22

I couldn't park in my driveway. In fact, I got the idea I'd never be able to park in my driveway again, unless I expanded it to wrap around to the back of my house.

Where my van usually sat was a brand new Ford F-250, shiny red with all the bells and whistles. But it wasn't the truck that made my mouth drop open and made me squeal with delight, it was what was attached to the hitch.

It was a trailer, but not just any trailer. It was a food-truck trailer complete with a fold-down bar top, stool seats for customers, and a Mugnaini wood-fired pizza oven. On the side of the trailer were bright red letters that said *Glenda, the Food Witch.*

I cried—as in blubbery mess ugly cry cried. No one had ever given me something so amazing, so incredible. I couldn't even begin to imagine how much all of this cost, or how much time and planning Xavier had put into getting this for me. When had he ordered it? He must have been planning this since our sandwich contest.

I examined the truck and the trailer, ooing and ahing over

how perfect everything was. Then realizing Xavier wasn't coming outside to meet me, I headed for the door.

Would he be inside? Naked and waiting for me in the bedroom as I'd hoped? Surely he'd gotten the subtext of what I'd wished for after the brisket contest. The truck and trailer were amazing, but what I *really* wanted was him.

As I went inside I realized the lights were already on. A demon stood inside my kitchen-that-was-the-whole house, elbows on the stainless steel table that we'd made love on just four days ago.

"Do you like it?" He asked softly, uncertainty in his eyes. "I wasn't sure if you wanted an oven to install here, or one for outside. Then I figured it would be really cool if you could make custom to-order pizzas from a food truck. It would give your business that extra that other caterers don't have. And maybe you could make slug pizzas for the gnomes to make up for the birthday party."

My heart leapt at the sight of him. "It's amazing. Beautiful. And the name on the side is…perfect." I squirmed. Now was the time to be courageous. What did I have to lose besides my pride?

"It's not what I *really* want though," I blurted out.

An unreadable expression flickered across his face. "You wanted the indoor pizza oven instead?"

"No." It was now or never. "I want the pizza oven you gave me earlier this week. I mean, I wanted us to…well, not just that." I took a deep breath. "I want you. I want you to stay here, to stay with me. I want you to cook with me, to be my friend, to be my lover, to hopefully be my everything, my bond-mate or whatever you demons call it."

He blinked, but remained silent.

"It wasn't your fault at all Xavier, and I'm so sorry for not trusting you, for not even letting you have a chance to explain," I went on. "There was a mix-up in the spices. Shelby gave me the wrong ones, and that's how the coriander got into the slugs. I jumped to conclusions. I automatically assumed you were at fault because you're a crossroads demon and I didn't trust you. Actually, I didn't trust me. I'd started to feel something for you, and I always fall in love with the wrong guys, the guys who don't care about me and disappoint me in the end. It was horrible of me to dump that baggage onto your shoulders, to believe you'd be like the others. I'm sorry, and I hope you'll forgive me and give me a chance to make it up to you."

His lips twitched. "Like you're going to make it up to the gnomes?"

I couldn't help but smile. "If you really want a wood-fired slug pizza, I'll make you one, but I was thinking of something else. If you're interested, that is."

He came around the stainless steel table, heading right for me. "Glenda, I'm happy to indulge in any wood-fired pizza you offer me, whether it's crust topped with slugs, or me topped with your gorgeous naked body."

"Then that's a yes?" I asked as he stopped inches from me. "You forgive me."

He bent and gave me a kiss, long and slow and so sexy my legs barely held me upright.

"That's a yes, my witch. And as for the rest…well, you did win our bet."

I suspected he'd thrown the bet, not wanting to force me into anything I might not want. And I knew that his saying "yes" to all I wanted had nothing to do with our bet. Still, a deal was a deal. I reached up and wound my arms around his neck, pulling him in for another kiss.

Then I dragged him off to bed to give him the best wood-fired pizza he'd ever experienced.

ABOUT THE AUTHOR

Debra lives in a little house in the woods of Maryland with her sons and two slobbery bloodhounds. On a good day, she jogs and horseback rides, hopefully managing to keep the horse between herself and the ground. Her only known super power is 'Identify Roadkill'.

For more information:
www.debradunbar.com
Debra Dunbar's Author page

ALSO BY DEBRA DUNBAR

Accidental Witches Series

Brimstone and Broomsticks

Warmongers and Wands

Death and Divination

Hell and Hexes

Minions and Magic

Fiends and Familiars (2019)

Devils and the Dead (2019)

White Lightning Series

Wooden Nickels

Bum's Rush

Clip Joint

Jake Walk

Trouble Boys

The Templar Series

Dead Rising

Last Breath

Bare Bones

Famine's Feast

Royal Blood

Dark Crossroads (Fall 2019)

* * *

IMP WORLD NOVELS

The Imp Series
A Demon Bound

Satan's Sword

Elven Blood

Devil's Paw

Imp Forsaken

Angel of Chaos

Kingdom of Lies

Exodus

Queen of the Damned

The Morning Star

* * *

Half-breed Series
Demons of Desire

Sins of the Flesh

Cornucopia

Unholy Pleasures

City of Lust

* * *

Imp World Novels
No Man's Land

Stolen Souls

Three Wishes

Northern Lights

Far From Center

Penance

* * *

<u>Northern Wolves</u>

Juneau to Kenai

Rogue

Winter Fae

Bad Seed

ACKNOWLEDGMENTS

Thanks to my copyeditor Jennifer Cosham whose eagle eyes catch all the typos and keep my comma problem in line, and to Renee George for cover design.

www.ingramcontent.com/pod-product-compliance
Lightning Source LLC
Chambersburg PA
CBHW050534190726
48284CB00003B/1069